My name is Callum Ormond.
I am sixteen
and I am a hunted fugitive . . .

CONSPIRACY 365

BOOK EIGHT: AUGUST

To Angie and Claire

Scholastic Australia
345 Pacific Highway
Lindfield NSW 2070
An imprint of Scholastic Australia Pty Limited
(ABN 11 000 614 577)
PO Box 579
Gosford NSW 2250
www.scholastic.com.au

Part of the Scholastic Group
Sydney • Auckland • New York • Toronto • London •
• New Delhi • Hong Kong • Puerto Rico

First published by Scholastic Australia in 2010.

Graphics by Nicole Leary.

Cover design by Natalie Winter.
Cover photography: boy by Wendell Levi Teodoro (www.zeduce.org)
© Scholastic Australia 2010; close-up of boy's face by Michael Bagnall
© Scholastic Australia 2010; person in straightjacket © photooiasson/
Shutterstock; underground tunnel © Perov Stanislav/Shutterstock.
Internal photography: spiky-haired boy on page 063 and 062
© istockphoto.com/Birgitte Magnus.

National Library of Australia Cataloguing-in-Publication entry:
Lord, Gabrielle, 1946-
Conspiracy 365: August / Gabrielle Lord.
ISBN 978-1-74169-320-1 (pbk.)
A823.3

ISBN-13:978-93-5103-682-1

Reprinted by Scholastic India Pvt. Ltd., July 2015, 2019

Printed at Shivam Offset Press, New Delhi.

CONSPIRACY 365

BOOK EIGHT: AUGUST

GABRIELLE LORD

SCHOLASTIC
SYDNEY AUCKLAND NEW YORK TORONTO LONDON
NEW DELHI HONG KONG PUERTO RICO

PREVIOUSLY ...

1 JULY

I gulp down a lungful of air as the fishing net I'm trapped in finally lifts out of the water. The boat crew hide me from the cops and I'm forced to work as a wheeler until the debt's paid off. When I'm helping a guy unload his fish into a freezer, a deckhand—who turns out to be Three-O from the attempted car jacking—locks me in the freezer so he can give me to the cops and claim the reward money. I'm desperate to escape before I freeze to death. I end up using Repro's track detonators to blast myself out.

3 JULY

Back at the beachside mansion my recurring nightmare of the white toy dog and wailing baby continues to taunt me.

8 JULY

Boges gives me an address—'Manresa' in Redcliffe—where I hope to find Great-aunt Millicent. Police presence on roads out of town has been increased which means it will be hard to get there.

9 JULY

Winter has overheard Sligo saying there is something written inside the Jewel. I confront her about the photo I found in Sligo's safe of her wearing the Jewel and she denies it's real, saying the image had to be digitally edited.

13 JULY

After narrowly escaping the cops, Zombrovski and Sligo at the train station, I begin my journey on a bus to Redcliffe. When I notice some guys looking at me, I get off and start making my way on foot, avoiding road blocks as I go.

18 JULY

Winter sends me a warning, saying Sligo has a lead on my location. I know I only have a short time to find my great-aunt. Manresa turns out to be a convent, and I'm told Millicent has taken another name—Sister Mary Perpetua—and that she hasn't spoken in twenty years. Straight away I start worrying that my trip has been for nothing . . . I call Boges and tell him about the writing on the Jewel. I spend the night in a dead nun's 'cell'.

19 JULY

I meet my great-aunt and to my shock she breaks her silence, mistaking me for her brother, Bartholomew. Apparently my dad contacted her about the Ormond Singularity before he died, but the family papers were put away in an envelope when she entered the convent. She warns me that the Ormond Singularity has meant the death of all who have tried to unravel it, and she also mentions a tragic set of twins—one returned safely, the other one lost . . . I locate the envelope in the convent archives and discover letters from Piers Ormond and a family tree.

20 JULY

Disturbed by a sound in the middle of the night I wander into the corridor and find Zombrovski sneaking around, dressed as a nun! He chases me through the convent and up the bell tower. With nowhere left to run, I'm trapped. Zombie shoves the massive bell towards me, but I lift my body out of its path, narrowly missing its force. The rebound momentum swings back towards Zombie, throwing him out of the tower, and sending him free-falling to the ground far below.

The fall was fatal—Zombie is dead. I grab my things and flee on a motorbike, gunning it through the crossfire of a shootout between Bruno and the police.

24 JULY

Back at the mansion, Boges and I catch up on what happened in Redcliffe. We go over the French script on the Jewel as well as Piers's letters. The solicitor whose name I couldn't remember contacts me on my blog!

25 JULY

I call the solicitor, Sheldrake Rathbone, and he tells me that he has Piers Ormond's will. He also has a client who wants confirmation that I have possession of the Jewel and the Riddle, in return for 'something of great importance'.

It's almost the anniversary of my dad's death, so Winter and I visit the Ormond mausoleum. She tells me more about the accident on her tenth birthday that took her parents' lives. She admits that it was her sneaking around Sligo's car yard months ago, looking for the car her parents had died in.

30 JULY

Oriana de la Force identifies herself on my blog as Rathbone's mysterious client. She urges me to meet him with the promise of Piers Ormond's will and information related to the twin baby abduction. Boges, Winter and I set up the meeting with Rathbone.

31 JULY

The three of us head to the arranged meeting place. As I enter the premises, alone, I realise I'm in a funeral parlour. I reach for the envelope waiting for me when the counter erupts and hits me on the forehead. Something sharp pierces my neck and I start to black out. I awake to find myself trapped inside a coffin. I sense myself being loaded into a hearse and driven to an unknown location. I can't move or scream. I feel the coffin being lowered into a grave, followed by the thudding sound of dirt being shovelled on top of it . . . It's my sixteenth birthday and I'm being buried alive.

1 AUGUST

153 days to go . . .

Unmarked grave, Infinity Gardens

12:00 am

Thud . . .

The thudding was becoming duller, more distant.

Thud . . .

The grave was being filled in, fast. The earth raining down on the lid of the coffin was building up an unbreakable barrier between me and the world of the living above.

I broke out in a cold sweat. I was being buried alive!

Thud . . .

I strained and struggled, terror and panic finally starting to overcome the effects of the drug they'd used to immobilise me. I tried to scream and kick and claw at the wooden walls, but it was useless. Fear destroyed all rationality, as I kept on thrashing—smashing my knees, elbows, fingers and head against the unyielding tomb.

Think, Cal, think.

Who said that?

Was I becoming delirious, hearing voices in my head?

Or was I hearing things because my brain was already shutting down, starved of oxygen?

Air. I needed to conserve air. Already, I was finding it hard to breathe. Struggling and panicking were consuming what little reserves there were.

I willed myself to be still.

The rhythmic thudding of shovels full of soil had stopped. Now it sounded like the dirt on top was being patted down.

Then that stopped too.

The job was over. They were done burying me.

I shook as I imagined the hearse driving away. I was in a desperate situation, but I needed to keep my head. I forced myself to breathe softly and lightly.

Again, I struggled uselessly, but then something vibrated near my hip.

My mobile!

How could they have left that on me? They must have thought that the drug they'd given me would keep me quiet . . . unconscious until I was dead. Or maybe they'd completely overlooked my mobile, tucked into my waistband, switched to 'silent'.

Please, Boges, I hope it's you calling, I said in my head. *Please stop this from happening! Please find me!*

In the tight, confined space, it was a struggle to reach my phone. I twisted and bent my elbow up awkwardly, then strained and stretched my fingers desperately. Finally my hand closed around it.

Then it stopped vibrating.

I'd been too slow! I'd missed it!

The air around my face and body felt hot. The air was thinning out. I held my phone, willing it to vibrate again.

I moved my sweating, trembling fingers until they rested on the loudspeaker button—I knew it would be too hard to get the phone up to my ear fast enough, and I didn't want to waste any more chances . . . if I was lucky enough to have another one come my way.

The instant my fingers felt the phone vibrating again, I hit the loudspeaker button.

'Dude! Where are you?' Boges's urgent voice reverberated around me. 'What have they done with you?'

'Boges, get me out of here!' I begged, faint with relief. 'Don't let me die down here!'

'Where are you?'

'I'm in a coffin! They've buried me! I don't know where I am, but please, get me out of here! I'm freaking out, man. Freaking out!'

Boges swore. Was I hallucinating again, or was that Winter's voice I heard crying out, 'Buried? He's been buried?'

The words coming out of my phone's loud-speaker were suddenly muffled. I couldn't make out what was being said.

'Boges! Winter!' I shouted. 'What's going on? Get me out of here! Please! I don't know how much longer I can last!'

'Tell us where you are!' Boges's voice returned, calling down a crackly line. I hoped the signal would hold up.

'I don't know where I am! I'm in a coffin, six feet under! I could be in a cemetery, but—' I paused, short of breath, and frustrated, 'I could be anywhere! All I know is that I'm underground!'

'OK, OK,' my friend repeated, trying to process what I was saying. Trying to figure out a way to save me.

'You have to help me! Did you see them drive off?' I asked, hoping Boges or Winter had seen the vehicle I'd been loaded into, back at the funeral parlour, and the direction it had taken. They had both promised they would be watching out for me when I went to meet Rathbone. 'Wherever they took me,' I added, 'there's a mound of fresh soil. And I'm under it!'

'We were watching Temperance Lane at both ends, and just after you went in we realised you were meeting Rathbone at a funeral parlour! We didn't see anyone coming, but after a while we saw a car—a hearse—leaving, sneaking along without any headlights on, and we tried to follow it . . .'

'Someone jumped me—they were hiding in one of the coffins, waiting for me. Whoever it was knocked me out, stuck me in a coffin, drove me away, and then buried me! You have to find me before I run out of air!'

'We will, I promise. There's a cemetery not far from where we are now. We're on our way!'

'But what if they took him somewhere else?' Winter's voice pleaded faintly in the background.

'We have to try!' Boges said back to her. The small amount of air in my terrifying prison was becoming thicker and hotter; I could feel my head swelling. 'Hang in there, Cal. Keep the line open. Cal? You there?'

'I'm not sure how much battery I have left. And I feel like I can't breathe properly.'

'Let's go! Boges, let's go!' Winter's voice screamed.

'We'll find you, I swear!' said Boges. 'Just hang

in there and stay calm. I have a program I can use to track your mobile and your location. You have to keep your phone on so the scanning program can home in on you. Try to take small, shallow breaths. You can survive in there for maybe thirty, forty minutes . . .'

'Just hurry, please . . .'

12:15 am

I felt like I was starting to hallucinate in the dark, hot box where I lay. Black and red misty demons seemed to dance in front of my eyes.

'Dude! Are you there?' called Boges. His voice was distorted. Was it me, or just my phone?

My heart was banging in my head and body, drumming a beat in my ears. I'd lost the Ormond Riddle and the Ormond Jewel. They'd been shoved into a coffin, just like me, and if Boges and Winter didn't find me soon, I'd be just another body in this hollowed ground, surrounded by the dead.

'Dude! Are you still with us?' begged Boges. 'Say something, please? Just say "yes".'

I wasn't sure if I was talking or just thinking the words. Turbulent voices twisted and thrashed against my skull. Could I really hear Boges's voice?

'We're looking for you right now, Cal! Just stay awake, OK!'

I knew that soon the oxygen sealed with me in the coffin would be replaced by the carbon dioxide I was breathing out. It would be lethal. I would die from my own toxic breath.

Unless my friends found me first.

12:19 am

I was hot, then cold. I seemed to come and go, lapsing in and out of consciousness. Clammy chills shuddered through me.

'Cal! Stay with us, we're on our way. I've activated the mobile phone scanner program on my laptop. Keep this line open. Hang in there, please buddy? Stay with me.'

12:26 am

'Cal, we're here! Your number's lighting up on my screen. Any minute now. Hang on! I can see a freshly dug grave! Winter, look! Over there!'

'Quick,' I croaked with renewed hope.

At last, they'd found me. I was almost sick with relief and terror all mashed together.

Then I heard Boges shout out again, and my heart faltered.

'Oh no! There's another one! And another one! There are loads of fresh graves in this place! What are we going to do? My program only gives us an approximate position. He's here somewhere . . .

What do we do, Winter? How are we going to know which one is his?'

'Boges, I don't know! We just have to start digging!'

'Cal? You there? You OK? Winter, he's not talking! He's not responding! How the hell can we know which pile he's under?'

I tried to speak, but I was too weak. My friends had come so close, and yet I was doomed to suffocate.

From somewhere, a long way off, I thought I heard Winter sobbing half-crazy words. 'Cal! I'm digging, I'll save you! Where are you? Yell out! Shout out! I need to hear your voice so I can find you!'

Half-conscious, I tried to open my mouth and call out to her. All that came out was a choking noise—the kind you make in a nightmare. Blackness swirled around me. Crazy patterns scrambled in the blackness in front of my eyes. I knew the lights were going out.

Then I thought I heard Boges's voice . . .

'Winter! We have to call for help! We can't do this, we have no choice. You can't dig him out . . . not with your bare hands . . . Stop it! Winter! Go to that phone box we saw across the road . . . I think his . . . battery's about to . . . about to die . . . Cal, if you can hear me,' he said to me, with a hazy voice like one from a dream, 'I'm so sorry. We really need help. We won't let you die. We can't do this alone. Cal? Cal? Winter's gone to call the police . . . I'm sorry, we have no choice. We need help . . . to get you out of there. But . . . if you can hear me and if you can manage it, somehow, try and lose the SIM card, Cal. Don't let anyone get their hands on it. Hang in there. We're going to get you out of there and we're all going to get back onto solving the DMO. See you again soon, OK buddy?'

I tried to answer him but darkness was closing in. The SIM card! With its record of all my phone calls, it would lead the police straight to Boges and Winter. After all they'd done for me I couldn't let them get caught. Any laws they'd broken, they'd broken for my sake only.

The phone cut out. Now I was completely alone. There was nothing but silence and the ghosts of the dead.

With every shallow breath I could feel myself slipping away. I fought to stay alert long enough to go over everything Boges had said. What could I possibly do about the SIM card? How could I lose the SIM card down here? There was nowhere to hide it. Unless . . .

I mustered all of my strength and concentration, and with weak fingers, I managed to fumble open the SIM card slot in my mobile. Slowly, despite the blood pounding in my ears and the shrieking noises that seemed to be coming from the centre of my brain, I struggled to move my hand, carefully clutching the card, to my lips. I poked my tongue out and pulled the card back into my mouth, then sucked it to the back of my throat.

My mouth was so dry, I didn't know if I could swallow it.

A whirlpool of blackness took me down.

2 AUGUST

152 days to go . . .

Room 3, Secure Wing
Armitage District Hospital

8:02 am

I tried to move, but my hands wouldn't obey me. I panicked, as the memory of being trapped underground in a coffin flooded back . . . was I still there? I suddenly recalled brilliant lights, and voices . . . Visions from a dying brain?

My sticky eyelids opened.

What?

I was no longer in a coffin! I was alive!

Grey light and mist surrounded me. I blinked, and blinked again. A foul taste filled my mouth; my throat felt swollen and raw.

I licked my dry lips and remembered attempting to swallow the SIM card. From the pain in my throat, I guessed it had gone down. I blinked again, squeezing my eyes to clear my vision.

The mist cleared. I spotted a glass of water beside me and instinctively went to pick it up. And that's when I realised why I still felt trapped—my hands were cuffed together in front of me with tough, white, nylon restraints.

And I was hooked up to some sort of drip or monitor by the bed.

I was in a *hospital*?

I was alive—I'd been saved. But now I was in custody?

The glass I'd reached for beside my bed was empty. I was in a small room, with a cupboard and a chair beside me, and a laboratory-style sink in the corner. The pale green walls and green vinyl squares on the floor reminded me of the intensive care unit Gabbi was in when I last saw her. The door in the wall opposite me had a small window in it.

There was a strong mix of anaesthetic vapours and disinfectant—that distinct hospital smell. I flopped back, exhausted and confused.

I had no memory of being saved. I must have lost consciousness when all the oxygen was used up in the coffin underground. But how did I get here?

I looked up and saw the steel bars on the tall windows, just like Leechwood Lodge Asylum. Now I knew for sure I was in some kind of police hospital or a locked ward in a normal hospital . . . for criminals.

Boges and Winter had somehow helped me cheat death, but by getting out of one terrifying situation, I'd ended up in another fix. I had no idea how I was going to get out of this one.

I hoped my friends weren't in trouble with the police for aiding and abetting a criminal. They were the only reason I was alive. Without them, Vulkan Sligo or Oriana de la Force would have done away with me by now.

8:13 am

I carefully swung my legs over the side of the bed, to try and get a glimpse of what was outside the window, but all I could see was another wall with windows in it just like the one I was looking out from. If I peered upwards, I could see a small square of sky. Even it looked grey and grimy. I shuffled over to the sink, trying carefully to avoid dislodging any of the cords around me, and banged the cold water tap on with my elbow. As I turned my head sideways to lean in and get a drink, something glinted, caught in the drain fitting. It was hard fishing it out with my tied hands but eventually my fingers closed around a small piece of flat metal. It was the larger half of a broken scalpel blade. Something like that could come in handy, I thought, so I took it back with me to the hospital bed, and slid it into a stitched pocket in the mattress.

I lay there staring at the ceiling panels, going over the last twenty-four hours. Who had tried to kill me? Who had leapt out of the coffin that I'd mistaken for a counter? And who had buried me? It was one thing to murder someone, but to try and take them out by burying them alive? What kind of monster was I dealing with?

That familiar scent I'd caught a whiff of when I was attacked was frustrating me . . . I couldn't place it. Did it belong to Oriana? Was it her perfume? Or Sligo's aftershave? My mind kept jumping from one question to the next, but I couldn't find any answers.

My thoughts were abruptly interrupted by the sound of a heavy lock unlatching. The door swung open and two men walked in. One was dressed in the pale green clothes of a nurse, and the other looked like a detective, wearing a dark suit under a beige overcoat and carrying a briefcase.

'God, the press was going crazy out there,' he said to the nurse, while smoothing down his hair. 'I've never seen so many photographers and journos in my life. It was like squeezing through a pack of wild animals. Bloody vultures.'

'He's conscious,' said the nurse, dismissively.

'I can see that,' he replied, sternly. He spun the chair beside the bed around and sat on it, then pulled a leather-backed wallet out of his pocket, flipping it open to show me his ID. 'Senior Sergeant Dorian McGrath,' he said, before snapping it shut again. 'Just so we both know who we are.'

McGrath had a narrow, shrewd face with wispy eyebrows above hazel eyes. Pale bristles shone on his jawline.

He stared at me while the nurse fussed and fumbled with a monitor nearby. McGrath seemed irritated, scowling in the nurse's direction, then turning his attention back to me.

'You're a very lucky boy, Callum Ormond. The doctors say just another minute or two down there and you would have suffered brain damage.'

McGrath slid his chair back, making a loud grating sound, and stood up. He stepped close to the bed and loomed over me, centimetres from my face. 'You've been one hell of a thorn in our sides, Ormond. You've done a lot of damage and you've wasted a lot of police hours. But now that we have you–' he paused to make a crushing movement with his fist, 'we want some answers.'

I kept my mouth shut. I wasn't going to tell him anything.

He moved in even closer to me. I could smell coffee on his stale breath.

His next question dropped on me like a bomb. 'What have you done with your sister?'

What?

'What have you done with your sister?' he repeated slowly and aggressively, spit flinging off his pursed lips.

Gabbi? Fear gripped me.

'You know, your sister, Gabbi Ormond,' he mocked. 'What do you know about her disappearance?'

Disappearance?

'My sister?' I whispered, shaken. 'What are you talking about? What's happened to her? She was at my uncle's house, being cared for. What do you mean, she's disappeared?'

The sergeant leaned away from me and frowned.

'They told me you were a top-notch liar, but I never would have believed it if I hadn't seen it for myself. They warned me you'd be convincing, said you can lie straight-faced and look like you're telling the truth, but you really are something else. Look,' he scoffed to the nurse who had been keeping to himself with a folder in the corner. 'The kid looks like he's going to cry!'

Anger surged through me. I jumped up, tried to rip my hands out of the restraints, but McGrath pushed me back, then sat down.

'What has happened to Gabbi? Has she been kidnapped?' I screamed at him. 'Tell me what has happened to my sister! I need to get out of here and save her! She's sick–what if the kidnappers don't know how to look after her?'

'Don't move, Ormond. Just answer my question. What have you done with her?'

'Listen to *me*! Answer *my* question! I know nothing! This is the first time I've even heard about it! I need to get out of here to save her. What's happened to her?!'

I tried to keep my voice steady, but I couldn't control it. The detective wasn't taking me seriously.

Dorian McGrath shifted in his seat. 'I can handle this,' he said to the nurse, who looked uneasy, like he was about to call security. 'Ormond. I know you're not working alone. An anonymous phone call came in last night, alerting us to where you were. Emergency Services suspected it was a hoax, but they sped to the scene, located you, and dug you out. We're very interested in the identity of the emergency caller.' McGrath opened his laptop, and switched it on. After a moment, he looked up at me, and turned the laptop a little. 'Listen to this.'

Suddenly a recording of Winter's distressed, sobbing voice cut through my tumultuous thoughts and into the grim air of my hospital room.

'Emergency Services? Oh thank God! Listen, you have to help me! Please! My friend, he's, he's been buried alive! These people put him in a coffin and buried him!'

'Calm down. Take a deep breath,' said the operator. 'Where is your friend? Are you nearby? Are you in danger?'

'Infinity Gardens! The cemetery! He's been buried here, in a coffin, but I don't know where! I need help! I've been digging, but I can't find him! There are a dozen fresh graves, and he's in one of them! He's going to die if we don't get to him soon!'

'You say he's in a coffin?' the operator asked dubiously. 'Is this some sort of prank gone wrong?'

'No, this is not a hoax! Or a prank! There are these people who are . . . Please, please just believe me! Please help! He's going to die if you don't come quickly! We need to dig him out! Send people with diggers! Fast! He's running out of oxygen! Please—'

Senior Sergeant Dorian McGrath stopped the recording.

In front of my boiling thoughts, I forced my face into an impassive mask. Winter's call had saved me, and I had to save her from being identified.

'Do you recognise that voice?' the sergeant asked.

I shook my head, trying to control my racing heart.

'Who cares!' I cried. 'I need to find my sister! Isn't that more important right now?'

'Once you get out of prison,' said McGrath, raising his eyebrows, 'you should go to Hollywood. Won't be for a hefty number of years, mind you,' he said with a sly smirk, 'but you sure are one convincing act.'

Fury and frustration spilled over. I tried to pull the restraints on my wrists apart but they seemed to just tighten, painfully.

'You're sitting there,' I yelled, my voice breaking, 'making stupid comments instead of getting out of here and searching for my sister! She's in a coma, for crying out loud! She needs twenty-four-hour care! I know you're not going to let me go, so *you* need to find her!' I stared at the sergeant's cynical face. He was convinced I was full of it. 'As if I have her!' I continued. 'Where do you think I've stashed her? Under this stinking mattress?'

It was no use. His face remained impassive.

'The girl who called us—your accomplice—who is she? Is she holding Gabbi?'

I glared at him, furious.

'I can see it's going to be a long day,' sighed the sergeant. 'Let's start at the beginning, shall we?'

10:44 am

He was on at me for ages, going over and over the same questions, trying to trick me into admitting that I'd taken Gabbi—that I knew where she was—that I had accomplices who were holding her while I was in captivity.

I was sick of hearing it.

'What you're suggesting is crazy,' I said, exhausted. 'Why would I take Gabbi? I can't look after her. Me? A fugitive? On the run, somehow managing an intensive care unit as well?'

'We don't think you took your sister to "look after her",' he snarled.

'You think I'd harm her? Is that what you think?'

'Why not? Finish what you started back in January,' he said bluntly. 'If we hadn't turned up that day, sending you running with our sirens blaring, I have no doubt you would have completed the job. We would have been carrying two dead bodies out of that house.'

'It *wasn't* me!' I yelled.

We were interrupted by another nurse with a tray of food and a drink. She looked nervous and couldn't look at me—her hands were shaking, making the juice in a plastic cup ripple.

'It's OK,' the sergeant said to her. 'Just put the food down and be on your way.'

She nodded towards him, put the tray down carefully, and then happily backed out of the room, leaving us behind.

On a plastic plate was a bowl of lumpy, greyish stew and some boiled carrots. I was thirsty, but I had no appetite. I was worried sick about Gabbi.

McGrath reached for the restraints on my wrists, holding out a huge, threatening pair of clippers.

'Can I trust you if I cut those off?'

'Probably not.'

'Ah, the first honest thing you've said all day!' The sergeant laughed before clipping the restraints and handing me the tray. 'You're nothing I can't handle.'

I picked up the plastic fork and poked one of the grey lumps. I quickly put the fork down again.

'Sergeant, please tell me what happened. Where were my mum and uncle when Gabbi was taken? They haven't been hurt, have they?'

He ignored my questions. 'Let's talk about something else,' he suggested. 'Why did you break into the undertakers' premises?'

'I didn't break in. The door was left open for me, just like Rathbone said it would be.'

'Rathbone?'

'It was all arranged by Mr Sheldrake Rathbone, our family solicitor. He organised the meeting. It was at his brother's place—the undertakers'. We were going to exchange information.' The sergeant was looking at me in disbelief again. I thought of something that might help my case. 'Check my blog and you'll see his message,' I said, hoping I wasn't about to put Winter in jeopardy by exposing her messages too. 'It was a private message. I'll give you access.'

'This is very tiring, Callum. Do you think we haven't already checked your blog? There's nothing there from a "Mr Rathbone". There aren't any private messages. You seem to be a mixture of cunning and stupidity. Why on earth would you expect us to believe that your family solicitor would be dealing with a criminal like you—unless he was advising you on how to best confess your crimes? Or preparing for your long-overdue court appearance? Anyway, back to the break-in. Was it just to steal money?'

'Steal money?'

'We found the money on you, Cal.'

'What are you talking about? They must have planted it on me! We need to get back to Gabbi!

Focus on her! You need to find her!'

'Nice one!' laughed McGrath, standing up and pacing around the room. '*You*, want *us* to find her.' He shook his head and ran his hands through his hair. 'You'd need to tell *me* what you've done with her first.' He spun around, fixing me with an angry glare. 'Where is she Cal?'

'You're wasting time on me!' I yelled. 'You're letting the real kidnappers get away! What do I have to say to convince you that I had nothing to do with it? You need two names, and two names only–Vulkan Sligo or Oriana de la Force. Rathbone is corrupt. He's working for Oriana. They're the ones who are responsible! You need to investigate them. They're after something I have. Something I *had*,' I corrected. 'They're the criminals! And they're ruthless! They're murderers!'

'Oh sure,' mocked McGrath, waving his hands in the air. 'Criminals are always running around pinching little girls in comas. You read about it every day. I've had it with your lies and games. I can't leave until I get the truth and all I'm getting from you is a whole lot of rubbish about criminals being after you. After *you*! *You're* the criminal! Give me a break!'

McGrath sat back down, leaning forward, his elbows on his knees.

'I'll tell you what we know already. We know

that you took your sister. Furthermore, we know that a short time later you broke into the premises of an undertaking business. Your own stupidity and criminal behaviour led to your accidental burial.'

Accidental burial! I shook my head slowly. How could I possibly convince him?

'You've already attempted to kill your sister—twice, actually. Once at the family home and later at the ICU in the hospital she was recovering in. If you cooperate and give us the name of your accomplice, or whoever has Gabbi right now—that is if she's still alive—I can make things easier for you. If you cooperate, I can have a word with the magistrate, and we can try for a shorter sentence.'

My own situation was bad enough, but somewhere, someone had Gabbi. Someone who didn't love her, or care for her safety. Someone who wanted to use her to get to me . . . or the rest of my family . . . what little was left of it. I couldn't bear to think what Mum was going through. I had been so happy Mum had taken Gabbi out of the hospital and set her up in Rafe's place, but she would have been safer if she'd stayed where she was. I clung onto the hope that the people who had Gabbi would figure it was in their interests to keep her alive.

'Please,' I begged, 'I might be able to find out

where she is. I'll cooperate—I'll work with you. You can keep me cuffed, although I promise I won't try to run away. My sister's life is more important to me than anything else in the world.'

The sergeant swore at me, then leaped up and violently grabbed me, his hands gripped on either side of my throat.

'Stop the bull, Ormond! You already know where she is,' he said, shaking me, 'because you took her! Dead or alive, you know full well where she is! You concoct this crazy story about solicitors and criminals being after you, chasing some fantastical nonsense. You're just trying to muddy the waters. But I've dealt with smarter crims than you, pal! And I make sure they go where they belong!'

'Get off me!' I demanded. 'Listen to me! My whole family has been in serious danger ever since my dad made a discovery about the Ormond Singularity when he was in Ireland. I'm the next in line—that's why people are trying to take me out, that's why I have to protect Gabbi. She's been taken to put pressure on *me*. They want to use her. To have bargaining power. Don't you understand? They want all the information I've gathered so they can use it together with all their money and power to solve the mystery!'

I was wasting my time. McGrath had a funny

half-smile on his face as if to say, *keep going, I'm enjoying this nonsense.*

'Why don't you make it easier for yourself and just tell me what really happened? We'll find out in the long run. Here's the deal: you tell me now, plead guilty when we charge you, and you'll get a reduced sentence. OK?'

'I've already told you I had nothing to do with Gabbi's disappearance. Rathbone contacted me on my blog and we arranged to meet at his brother's place in Temperance Lane to exchange information. I had something he wanted, and he had something I wanted. He was acting as a go-between for Oriana de la Force. I went there at the time we agreed, and then someone attacked me, knocked me out, and I wound up six feet under.'

'Sure, sure,' he said. 'Let's see if I have it right. Two leading members of the city's legal fraternity elect to meet up with a violent young offender in an undertakers' business. Let's not forget that the message you claim Mr Rathbone sent you has mysteriously vanished from your blog. And it was all a complicated set-up to kill you. You really expect me to swallow that?'

The way he put it, and the superior sneer on his face, made it sound pretty unbelievable.

There was a knock at the door. A policewoman entered the room and passed a sheet of paper to the sergeant. He paused by the door to look at it.

'You might be interested to hear this, Callum. Here is the sworn statement of Mr Enfield Rathbone, undertaker and brother of Sheldrake Rathbone, solicitor. Have a read of it.'

1 August

My name is Enfield Alan Rathbone. I was asleep at home when Senior Sergeant Dorian McGrath called me to say that he needed me to come down to the Richmond Bay Police Station to help him with his enquiries into a critical incident, involving the wrongful burial of a person by my firm of undertakers, Rathbone, Greaves and Diggory of 317 Temperance Lane.

When the police escorted me to my undertaking premises in the very early morning of 1 August, I first saw that the back door had been forced open. What followed was the discovery of further damage to my shop–broken shelving, damaged coffins and smashed urns, torn curtains– and the theft of a relatively small amount of money from our cash drawer.

It is my understanding that someone, whom I now know to be Callum Ormond, broke into the premises to steal money, or jewellery from the deceased, and perhaps find a quiet, comfortable place to sleep for the night. It appears that after he took what he could, he crawled into one of our top-of-the-range coffins that was stored in the rear of the shop—the Presidential Candidate—oak and red-cedar veneer with silver plate fittings and high-quality satin lining. It was there that he fell asleep. Our contractors arrived shortly after to collect another Presidential Candidate coffin that contained the remains of the recently deceased Stanley Marius Smedley, an ex-convict whose relatives wished him to be buried privately.

Unfortunately they picked up the wrong one, containing Ormond, and they conveyed the coffin to the hearse and proceeded to the cemetery and then the burial. Why he didn't wake up and alert them to his presence, I do not know. Perhaps he was inebriated, perhaps he bumped his head when attempting to search high shelving for our safe . . . Regardless of the reason, this was the only burial we had contracted to carry out on 31 July.

I am shocked that such a thing could happen. Nothing like this has happened to our firm before and we have been established since 1911.

Enfield Alan Rathbone

I looked up from the statement. Sergeant McGrath was eyeballing me. 'So what do you have to say about that?'

'Lies! All lies! I went there to meet *Sheldrake* Rathbone! I was waiting for him when someone knocked me out. All I know is that I woke up in a coffin, and before I could do anything about it, I was six feet under!'

'You don't deny you were in a coffin–'

'I've never denied that. But I didn't voluntarily get in there!' I shuddered, recalling the claustrophobic terror. 'Someone knocked me out and then drugged me or something. When I woke up I could hardly move, or say a word. It was all hazy. Test my blood! I promise you'll find something sinister in my system!'

'We've already had the toxicology results on your blood tests rushed through the lab. There is no evidence of any drug in your system to support your statement.'

'Then they used something that disappears quickly! Everyone's heard of drugs like that!'

McGrath took the statement back from me, folded it and slipped it into his briefcase. 'This is your last chance to tell me where we can find Gabbi.'

I knew it was no use pleading my case. Nothing I said was going to be taken seriously.

'You do understand the serious nature of the charges against you?'

I ignored him again.

'I'm leaving,' said McGrath. 'You have refused to cooperate.'

'How do you expect me to cooperate?' I shouted, fury and frustration burning wildly inside. 'I can't own up to things I didn't do! You should stop wasting crucial time on me and investigate the people I've told you about. Investigate de la Force and Sligo! Investigate Rathbone! Get out there and do your job, why don't you? Find my sister!'

I made a desperate lunge, but McGrath moved swiftly, grabbing me before I made it anywhere near the door, and with a painful twist to my wrists, he threw me with such force onto the hospital bed that I crashed heavily to the floor on the other side. My drip ripped out and snaked around for a second like a wild hose.

McGrath wrenched me back up onto the bed and pounced on me, pulling more restraints out.

'Callum Thomas Ormond, I'm arresting you on two counts of attempted murder. You don't have to say anything, but anything you do say could be taken down and used in evidence against you. Do you understand?'

5 AUGUST

149 days to go . . .

4:00 pm

I stared at the cop through the small square window in the door of my secure hospital room. He sat there bored, diagonally opposite my door on a chair in the corridor outside. Sometimes he'd stand up and walk around or chat to the nurses as they came by. Occasionally he'd peer through the window.

A nurse would come in intermittently to check my blood pressure and the monitors I was again hooked up to. I knew it wouldn't be long before I'd be transferred out of the hospital and into prison.

At the very time when I needed to be out searching desperately for Gabbi, I was stuck in this place where the hours dragged on painfully slowly. Every second that ticked by meant more danger for my sister. I didn't want to think about it.

I could feel the pressure of the hopeless

situation I was in building inside me, and started to do something methodical to distract myself—counting the ceiling panels above me. There were twelve of them—white rectangles held in place by ceiling batons. One of them in the corner over the wash basin was a little crooked and not properly aligned like the others. For some reason it really got on my nerves. My line of sight kept going back to it.

I couldn't believe that with everything going on, I was irritated by a crooked ceiling panel.

6 AUGUST

148 days to go . . .

10:32 am

Overpowering fear and worry about Gabbi had me pacing the room, desperately looking around for an escape. Together with the loss of the Ormond Riddle and the Ormond Jewel, and the long hours of boredom, it took everything I had not to start kicking the door and screaming my head off.

But the days I'd spent in this room had helped me get clear about one thing: I had to get away from this hospital. Once they put me into the prison system, locked up in a remand centre awaiting trial, I knew there'd be no bail for me. It would be much harder for me to escape then, than now. This secure ward in the hospital was my best bet.

I had to find Gabbi. Someone had to save her. Retrieving my backpack—containing the Jewel and the Riddle—could wait. Right now my sister was all that mattered.

12:25 pm

A tall nurse entered my room and placed a meal tray down on the small table beside my bed. This time the grey stew had a pile of green peas beside it.

I held my restrained wrists up to her.

'Forget it,' she said. 'Just like last night and this morning, they're staying on.'

She left and I awkwardly forced a couple of mouthfuls of the slop down, then fell back on my bed.

1:31 pm

I lay there staring at the crooked ceiling panel. This empty time was forcing me to put things together in my head. Sheldrake Rathbone must have been more than just an intermediary between me and Oriana. Maybe he'd always been her greedy partner in crime. Being the family solicitor meant that he had access to all the family documents relating to the Ormond Singularity, and he could have handed everything over to her. But then again, he might have been bribed or threatened by Oriana into helping her trap me.

Had there ever been anything in that envelope, or was the entire thing a set-up? Was there anything to find out about the twins . . . or was that all a pile of rubbish? I was feeling really stupid. I saw now how the idea of a second meeting—with

Oriana—had worked psychologically on me, made me less vigilant about the first meeting, with Rathbone. I'd fallen into their trap like a fool. I'd been blinded by my own hope of getting hold of the Piers Ormond will, and finally uncovering the truth about my past.

Boges and Winter too, both normally suspicious when it came to trusting anyone, had also been caught up in the excitement of finally getting more info. The three of us together had felt like an unstoppable trio.

I groaned aloud. Oriana had the Riddle back and now, thanks to me, she had the Jewel too. Both halves of the double-key code. Plus she had everything else she needed to solve the Ormond Singularity. She had money, influence, power . . . freedom. All the things I didn't have. I could've pulled my hair out in aggravation.

I jumped up and walked around the room. The IV tugged on my forearm as my brain surged with fears about Gabbi and frustration over my careless decisions.

4:58 pm

Faint, but familiar, voices outside my door propelled me to my feet.

I squashed my ear up against the thick door, straining to listen.

'Now, Win, please try and stay calm,' said a voice belonging to someone I knew too well—it was Uncle Rafe, talking to my mum! 'Going in there and shouting at him about Gab,' he continued, 'isn't going to help us get to her any faster. We need him to cooperate. OK, love?'

Love? Since when did Rafe use words like 'love'?

'Whatever you think is best,' said my mum.

'And if at any moment it gets too hard for you, we can leave. You just say the word.'

'That's right,' Sergeant McGrath's gruff voice added. 'His hands are restrained, and we're here if he's stupid enough to try and pull a swift one.'

Their footsteps approached and I jumped back to my bed, fidgeting nervously with my bound hands.

The door opened and Mum and Rafe walked in together, accompanied by the sergeant and the corridor police guard.

Mum wouldn't look at me. She kept her head down, eyes on the ground.

'Hello Cal,' said Rafe.

'Rafe,' I said, acknowledging him.

'Callum, your family is here to speak with you,' McGrath announced. 'We'll leave you alone for a short while,' he said to Rafe, 'but we will both be just outside the door should you need us.'

With that, he and the corridor cop left the room.

My mum suddenly made a move towards me, then faltered. Rafe had his arm around her, restraining her, guiding her to the chair near the bed instead. I couldn't tell whether she'd wanted to rush to me to hug me . . . or to hit me.

'Sit down, Win,' he said, flashing me a look of grave concern.

Mum sat down awkwardly. She had lost a lot of weight and there were hollows around her eyes that weren't there before. She looked really frail. Rafe, too, looked run-down and weary. His hair was now heaps more silvery than dark.

'Cal,' said Mum, hesitantly, glancing up at Rafe as she spoke, 'I don't know what to say to you.'

'You could start,' I said, 'by telling me what happened to Gabbi, and how in the world she was kidnapped from under both of your noses.'

I could see Rafe's jaw clench and his lips tense and contort with anger. He cleared his throat.

'Cal, we were hoping that you would be able to tell us that.' He took a deep breath and looked at my mum and then back to me. 'Even though your mother doesn't approve of it, I'm taking out a mortgage on the house, to raise money for your defence. Now that you're finally back with us—now that you've been incarcerated—we want you to have the very best lawyers money can buy. But first,' he said before pausing, 'you have to tell us what you've done with Gabbi.'

Mum's hand reached out for Rafe's. She squeezed it tight—the knuckles on her thin fingers whitening. Then she leaned into him and began to cry.

I stared silently at them. I couldn't speak.

'We've had discussions about this, and your mother and I both believe that there is some kind of insanity at work. If we can build up a case of diminished responsibility—that you're not in your right mind when you do these things—you might not have to go to prison.'

'Please, Cal,' my mother moaned, 'just tell us what you've done with her. I'm begging you. She has done nothing to you except love you. Please stop punishing her and let her come home. She's just a kid . . .'

I was gutted. They genuinely thought I was mad. I glared at both of them in disbelief.

'You think I'm crazy,' I said, shaking my head. 'But I'm not! You *must* know that I would never do anything to hurt Gabbi. I didn't hurt her the first time and I sure haven't done anything to her since. I don't know what to say to make you believe me, Mum. Dad warned me danger could be coming, and he was right. But all I've been trying to do is stay alive and clear my name so we can all be together again. I haven't seen Gabbi since that day in the ICU. And that was when I was trying to stop you from turning her life support off! Why would I hurt her? Why would I kidnap her?'

'Stop lying to me,' said Mum, turning tear-filled eyes on me. 'The police confirmed that your DNA was found at the scene—on the window frame, on Gabbi's bed, on the furniture in the room. Everywhere, Cal!'

I remembered how I'd run through all the rooms at my uncle's place, back in January, desperately searching for the drawings Dad had addressed to me. I'd touched so many drawers and cupboards, leaving DNA everywhere.

'That's because I went to Rafe's place, back in January—'

'You what?' asked Rafe. 'What were you doing at my place on your own? How did you get in?' Rafe stared hard at me. 'Well?'

I'd already said too much. I should have kept my stupid mouth shut.

'Oh, no,' cried Mum, 'don't tell me you've broken into Rafe's place before!'

'It wasn't like that, I swear!' I pleaded. 'You have to believe me, Mum! I'm innocent! The public can think what they want, but I need you to believe me!'

'Oh, Cal, I always hoped and prayed you'd turn out OK. In spite–'

'In spite of what? What happened to me, Mum, to make you think I could turn into a monster? Tell me! Tell me now! I have a right to know!'

'What's going on in here?' barked McGrath, alerted by our raised voices. 'Settle down, Ormond. You OK?' he asked Rafe and my mum.

'We're fine, Sergeant,' replied Rafe, through gritted teeth. 'Perfectly fine.'

McGrath nodded and backed out of the room slowly and suspiciously.

Mum's eyes were turned away from me again. I knew she was distressed, but I couldn't forgive her for not believing me, and keeping me in the dark about my mysterious past. She was my mum. She was supposed to stick by me.

I jumped off the bed. They both flinched but I didn't care. I turned to face them.

'I've heard of *serial killers* whose mothers still support them.'

I tried to read the expression in Mum's eyes, but they seemed strangely foreign to me. It was a peculiar sensation–as if she wasn't really there behind them, but was trying, unsuccessfully, to connect with me.

'Why can't I get through to you, Mum? Stop wasting your time chasing me, when the real crims are on the loose out there! Why won't you believe me when I tell you that I had nothing to do with the bad things that have happened to Gab? What has happened to *you*?'

'That's quite enough,' snapped Rafe. 'Don't speak to your mother like that. If you really cared for her, you would answer her question. She feels like she's already lost you. Don't be responsible for her losing Gabbi as well.'

I studied my mum's face. There was definitely something different about her. Like something had broken in her mind.

'Please Cal. Please tell us what you've done with Gabbi,' said Rafe. 'Please, we just want her back home, safely.'

'Mum,' I said softly, 'I really understand what you've been through. I've been through it too! But you mustn't let it destroy your trust in me. I'm still the same Cal.' I paused then, because what I'd just said wasn't really true any more.

Something stirred deep in my mind—a warning. *You are overlooking a very important connection,* said a tiny voice. Like when I'd first seen the key with the black tag thrown on Rafe's bed, and couldn't recall what it unlocked. Now, I tried to reach back into my memory for it, but in a flash it was gone. For a crazy moment, I wondered if the guy who looked just like me had something to do with Gabbi's disappearance.

'Please, Cal. I'm begging you,' said my mother, gripping Rafe's hand, her knuckles white once more. 'Tell us where she is.'

Rafe looked at Mum before he spoke. 'Cal, there is a freshly deposited layer of DNA in Gabbi's room that belongs to you. That means you were the last person there, so there is no point in lying to us. It's only going to earn you more time behind bars. Please consider your poor mother and do everything you can to cooperate with the police investigation. Before it's too late . . .'

'There's this guy,' I said, tentatively, 'that I've seen around the city a couple of times. He looks exactly like me.' I searched my mother's face, desperate for an answer, desperate to find some sort of recognition in her eyes. 'Mum,' I pleaded, 'could I have a twin?'

Just as I finished the last word, Rafe pounced on me. Mum jumped up from her chair, crying.

'Stop it!' I yelled as Rafe shook me. 'Get off me!'

'No, *you* stop it! These lies! And now some crazy nonsense about a twin! You're sick, boy!

Sick! How can you distress your mother like this? Can't you see you're breaking her heart? We just want to know our Gabbi's OK!'

I felt his fingers closing around my throat, and heard my mother screaming as he shook me as hard as he could. I struggled uselessly, hindered by the wrist restraints.

Within seconds the police officer who'd left the room raced in again and hauled Rafe off me. 'Calm down, mate,' he said. 'Take it easy. I understand how you feel, but you can't be jumping on the kid like that.' He shot me a filthy look. 'He'll be safely locked up in the remand centre tomorrow.'

Rafe pulled himself together, straightening his tie and smoothing his hair down. His eyes had welled up with tears—something I'd never seen happen to him before. For a moment his face reminded me of Dad.

'I'm sorry, officer,' he said. 'I let my feelings run away with me. It's the boy's mother I'm concerned about. She's been through so much. Too much for one person. We just hoped that Cal would . . . would . . . I don't know. Gab's been missing for days now. It's been too long. Come on, Win. Let's go. I don't want him upsetting you any more.'

Rafe put his arm around my mum and began

guiding her out of my room. I wanted to cry like a baby. I wondered if the people who were trying to destroy our family had made a start on my mum as well. As if someone had cursed her. Crushed her spirit, and left a changeling in her place.

'Please, darling,' said my mother with tears in her eyes, turning back as she left. 'Please, Cal, where is my daughter?'

Her desperate wailing trailed off as she and Rafe left me behind. Alone again.

Once upon a time, this might have broken my heart. But not now–not after all I'd been through. Over seven months on the street, surviving day by day, had made me tougher. If my mother believed these terrible things about me, then I didn't need her.

Words suddenly spilled out of me; I shouted them into the empty air: 'I'm going to prove to you that you're totally wrong about me! I don't know how I'm going to do that right now, but I'm promising you that I'll get Gabbi back and then maybe you'll realise how badly you've treated me!'

10:36 pm

I leaned over to read the clipboard hanging off the end of my bed.

DISTRICT ARMITAGE HOSPITAL

SECURE WING

Rm 3

Patient awaiting transport to
Remand Centre

Name: Callum Ormond, 16 years.
Arrested on suspicion of attempted
murder and kidnapping.

Notes: Violent, irrational episodes.
Paranoia increasing. Must be kept
in locked wards at all times.
Particular care at handover times.
Requires security assistance with
transport to Remand.

No grey stew that night for dinner; instead I was given a piece of rubbery white material that once might have been part of a fish, surrounded by a mixture of carrots and peas. It was my last night at the hospital. Tonight would be my last chance of escape. My last chance of saving my sister. I had to think of a way out.

I stared up at the crooked panel in the ceiling. And that's when I thought of something that just might work. But first, I had to free my hands.

10:50 pm

I felt around the mattress for the piece of scalpel blade I'd hidden, and almost cut my fingertip off when I found it. I figured if I could wedge it somewhere securely, I could cut through the nylon bands that tied my hands.

The timber of the window sill was a little weathered and cracked. Pushing carefully so as not to cut myself, and using a face cloth to protect my fingers, I forced one end of the broken blade down into a split in the wood. This left part of the blade fixed at an angle like a tiny bayonet. I pushed it to test it. It remained firm, tightly wedged into the timber. I dragged the chair over and sat down next to the window. It was going to take a while to carefully cut through.

From time to time, I peered around to check

the little window in my door, occasionally walking over to see what was going on in the corridor. In his seat across the hall from me, the cop who was supposed to be guarding me sprawled, head back, mouth open and eyes shut.

It was a long and painful process. Sometimes I'd slip, and cut my hands, and after an hour or so, I had quite a sore, raw wound on the side of my wrist.

I kept at it. I had nothing to lose.

It was hard to see what I was doing in the dim light from the corridor but finally, I was able to snap through the nylon. One cuff fell to the floor; the other remained like a bracelet around my wrist. I was free. At least, my hands were free.

I pulled out my drip and bandaged my injured wrist with part of the top of my hospital pyjamas, tying it off with a knot. Then I quickly changed into my clothes from where they'd been folded in the cupboard beside the bed, and stepped into a pair of canvas and rubber hospital slippers.

After checking that my guard was still dozing in the corridor, I started a close inspection of the ceiling panels. The crooked panel was one of those that ran along the wall, and directly under it was the basin. Just above that were two steel brackets that held a narrow, wooden shelf on which stood soap and toothbrushes. If I could trust the two steel brackets to hold my weight, I could reach the ceiling and swing myself up into it . . .

7 AUGUST

147 days to go . . .

12:05 am

The thought of escape had filled me with adrenaline and excitement. 'Hang on, Gabs,' I whispered, preparing for the next part of my escape plan. 'I'm coming for you.'

Moving silently, I glided to check the door. The corridor cop had woken and now was a few metres away up the hallway, leaning against the counter at the nurses' station. He was chatting to the night sister. This was my only chance.

Although the light in my room was off, light from the corridor shone in, enough for me to see by. I tiptoed over to the sink and basin, silently putting a chair beside it.

I climbed up on the chair and then tentatively put one foot in the sink, slowly transferring more weight into it. The basin held, but this was only half my weight. If it smashed under me, not only would it bring everyone running and put an end to my escape plan, but the broken ceramic of the sink could cut like glass, and open my leg right up.

I took my foot out of the sink and climbed down for a minute, shoving the seat of the chair under the sink, hoping that it would give some support if the sink cracked. I took the thin piece of wooden shelving off the brackets and quietly laid it under the bed.

'This is it,' I told myself, using the back of the chair to climb up next to the sink again. This time, moving as quickly as I could, and only using the sink as a brief foothold, I got one foot on one bracket and lunged towards the ceiling.

Feeling around for the other bracket with my other foot, I found it, and pressed flat against the wall. I slowly straightened up. I held my breath.

The brackets held.

I straightened my legs, reaching for the tiny gap between the crooked ceiling panel and the wall.

The bracket under my left foot suddenly gave way. I had no time to lose. As I regained my balance on the remaining bracket, my right hand grasped the timber joist that I could see through the small gap in the crooked ceiling panel.

The second bracket gave under me, leaving me dangling like a gibbon. Surely the cop outside my room would have heard that.

I swung for a few more seconds, listening for voices outside the room. There were voices—that of the cop and the night nurse—and they were talking and laughing quite loudly, completely unaware of what I was up to. That was why the copper hadn't noticed the crunching sounds made by each of the brackets as they came away from the wall.

I prepared to pull myself up.

With a loud creak, the door to my room suddenly started swinging open. I didn't wait to see who my visitor was!

My body galvanised in an upwards dive, and I grabbed the ceiling joist with both hands, hauling myself up, bashing the crooked ceiling panel aside with my head and shoulders as I pulled myself into the roof space.

Instinctively, I grabbed a beam above my head with one hand, while I squatted, my legs straddling two ceiling joists, avoiding stepping on the thin plasterboard panels that I was sure would collapse under even part of my weight. I nudged the ceiling panel back into position with my free hand.

There was a small crack through which I could see a tiny section of the room beneath me.

The lights switched on. I sensed, rather than saw, people running into my room, and heard their agitated voices.

'He's not here!'

'Well, where is he?'

'Maybe the doctors took him? Or the police? Was he collected by Remand already?'

'No! He's escaped!'

'Call security! And call for back-up!'

It would only be seconds before they noticed the damaged wall brackets and worked out where I'd gone. I had to move quickly. And carefully.

12:19 am

Crouched in the dark ceiling space I looked around in the murky light that shone through tiny cracks in the roof.

'He must have slipped past us somehow.'

'No way. The door was locked and his hands were tied. And I've been on guard out here for hours.'

'Look, he's busted the shelf brackets!'

'Must have been looking for something to use as a weapon!'

'This ward is locked. He can't have gone far,' one voice claimed desperately.

'Oh God,' said the corridor cop, with a strong sense of dread. 'Here comes trouble.'

Someone new stormed into the room, with a voice full of authority and anger. 'I want that adolescent psychopath found immediately and I want him escorted to the Remand Centre! I want him out of my hospital! Now! Do you understand? Find him, cuff him, and get him out!'

They hadn't worked out how I'd disappeared, or where to, yet. But it was only a matter of time before they'd realise I was somewhere in the dark and dusty ceiling above them.

I scrambled through the roof cavity as quickly as I could, stepping from joist to joist. After a while I came across another loose ceiling panel and paused to look through and get my bearings. I could just make out the reception area.

I peered through, quiet and still.

A cop with a familiar, agitated swagger was pacing across the open space just in front of the main entrance to the hospital foyer.

He turned and I caught a glimpse of his face . . .

Kelvin!

What the heck was Kelvin doing here? Decked out as a cop?

Oriana de la Force had what she wanted, so why had she sent one of her assassins? Surely she had everything she needed from me already!

Whatever the answer was, it was more reason for me to get out of this place where I was a sitting duck.

I had to move fast. I remembered a movie I'd seen where this guy had used the air conditioning ducts to wriggle through. I had no idea if this was possible or not, outside of Hollywood, but I had to try. Running along the wall around me was the long, square, aluminium ducting, and at the end of it, facing me, was the big exhaust fan, covered in wire caging. The ducting looked wide enough to fit me inside, if I could just get in there and start crawling. The exhaust fan would have to be my entry point.

I had no tools. All I had were my hands, one of them with painful cuts.

Crawling along the narrow joist, I made my way to the cage. Now that my eyes had adjusted to the dark better, I stared at the intimidating trio of fan blades that sliced around the opening of the duct. They were moving slow enough for me to make out the number of blades, but fast enough to take my head off.

The cage covering was secured by four clips, one near each corner. It didn't take me long to undo them. That was the first problem out of the way.

The blades spun, unobscured in front of me. They suddenly seemed more powerful and sharper. I looked around, frantic for an idea on how to get past them.

There were four thick metal joins—parts that connected the exhaust fan to the ducting—around the inside rim, just behind the blades. I needed to try and find something to wedge in between one of the joins and a blade, to stop them all from spinning.

My shoe! I ripped one of my canvas shoes off, almost losing my balance and tumbling onto one of the thin ceiling panels in the process.

I held the shoe out, trembling in my hand. I had to get the timing right, or I'd mess it up and make a whole lot of noise, signalling my location to security. Blowing all hope of escape. And all hope of finding Gabbi.

Or I could lose my hand.

I watched the blades go around, around, around . . .

Here goes!

Swiftly, I tossed the shoe in.

It bounced around a bit, and I cringed at the noise it was making, but then it stopped beside one of the joins, as I'd hoped, and the blade hit it. It stopped!

Unable to continue spinning, the blades hummed and groaned, like they were desperate to keep going, desperate to fight whatever had stopped them.

The commotion in the hospital below was increasing. There was no time to lose. I crawled into the space between the blades, praying I wouldn't dislodge the shoe that was keeping me in one piece.

12:26 am

I squeezed through the narrow gap and crawled into the opening of the square duct. I turned back, amazed I'd made it, then jerked my shoe back out. The blades quickly started spinning once more, picking up speed with every second. I slipped my beaten-up shoe back on.

Ahead of me, the length of the duct was pitch black. I began worming my way ahead, hoping the aluminium labyrinth was strong enough to hold my weight. I had no idea where the tunnels would lead, or where I should go. My plan was to just get out of the secured area of the hospital. Maybe if I could find my way to another part of the hospital, I'd have a chance of getting out unseen.

My heart started racing uncontrollably. For a minute I felt like I was trapped inside the claustrophobic walls of the coffin again. I gulped air down, reminding myself that I could breathe as much as I liked.

A sudden roar made me jump. The air conditioner had kicked up a notch in power, like it was on an automatic timer, and a rush of air blew dust up into my nose and eyes. Air whistled past my ears, but I put my head down and shut my eyes—it was too dark to see ahead anyway—and I kept crawling along, forcing my way ahead.

I swung a hard right when I reached a corner, carefully manoeuvring my body around the bend. Ahead the air carried the faint scent of coffee and food and, further along the tunnel, I could see light.

I came to a large grille—some sort of lightweight filter. Through the mesh, I peered cautiously into the room beneath me. A long table was visible, surrounded by chairs, its surface partially covered by magazines and coffee mugs. It looked like a staff room, but luckily for me it was completely empty.

It didn't take much effort to prise the grille up. I couldn't wait to get out of the confined space. As I pushed the grille to the other side of the opening, a shower of dust fell onto the table below. I must have been covered in dirt.

I lowered myself through the hole and into the room as far as I could, and then let go of the duct, landing on my feet on top of the table.

Quickly I jumped to the ground and ran for cover beside a tall cupboard, up against a wall.

I tried to shake some of the dust off my clothes, and wiped my face on my sleeve. So far, luck had been with me. But I couldn't expect it to last.

Not far from my position, thudding feet were running up and down the corridors, voices were panicked and shouting. No doubt the staff were on high alert, wary of the criminal on the loose in the hospital. But they still mustn't have realised I'd escaped through the ceiling, otherwise they'd be on me in a flash.

Desperate for an idea on my next step, I pulled open one of the cupboard doors. A row of nurses' uniforms hung inside. My good luck was continuing! I wrenched out a pale-green shirt and pants, and pulled them on over my clothes. I ran my hands through my hair and took a deep breath.

12:40 am

Standing tall and straight, and walking with a confident stride, I made my way down the corridor, past dark wards with occasional pools of light over individual beds, past a nurses' station where two ladies were engaged in deep conversation, discussing a patient's medication, and past a security guard talking very seriously into his walkie-talkie. He didn't even look up as I walked by.

I sidled into a lift and rode to the ground floor, dreading what I was going to find there. I braced myself when the lift doors parted.

Before me was an elderly guy snoring in a wheelchair, being wheeled by a woman who appeared to be his wife. I stepped out, and while holding the lift doors open for them, I used the opportunity to scan the ground floor, left and right.

There were cops in both directions. But there was only a matter of ten or so metres between me and the exit. Somehow I needed to just make it past the cops.

'Thanks, dear,' said the woman. 'Actually,' she said, backing out of the lift, 'would you be an angel and mind him here for a minute or two while I duck into the ladies? Something's going on in this place, and it's making me nervous! There are too many policemen and women around for this hour of the night,' she said with a chuckle.

'Sure,' I said, taking over the handles from her.

She smiled, then toddled down the hallway towards the toilets. I grasped the wheelchair firmly and steered it away in the opposite direction. This would be the perfect cover to get me to the exit.

I wheeled the snoring old gentleman casually past the reception area and towards the large, automatic double doors that led to freedom outside.

I passed the cops without any trouble. There

were five or six of them, huddled in a circle, busy making some sort of plan of attack . . . and all the while, letting their prey walk right on by.

When I reached the exit I turned the wheelchair around and parked it, before silently thanking the old guy asleep in it for the help he'd unknowingly given me.

Through the glass that separated me from outside, the bright lights of the hospital lit up a large circle surrounding the building and the stairs. Just beyond that, half-hidden in the shadows of the night, a line of cops waited. Their distinct silhouettes revealed that they were armed, in position and ready to attack.

For a second I thought about backtracking and finding another exit, but a quick look behind me showed that the cops I'd just passed were on the move—in my direction.

I took another deep breath and stepped outside the doors. I just had to reach the cover of darkness. How? I had no idea.

1:03 am

I pretended to look down at a non-existent watch on my wrist, in the hope that I could pass as an exhausted nurse leaving a late shift. There was a small gap between the line of cops and the reserved parking area, so I made a beeline for it.

I could sense one or two of the officers stirring, looking up to check me out. But it was when I only had a few steps left to go to reach the corner that I walked straight into Kelvin.

Kelvin!

'Look out,' he grunted before sidestepping, and moving on up the stairs, heading back into the hospital. He hadn't recognised me.

I took another step down, preparing to jump and run for it, when I heard Kelvin's roar from just a couple of metres behind me.

'It's *you!*' he yelled. His footsteps instantly pounded back down the stairs after me.

I deftly jumped aside to dodge his grip as he tried to leap out and tackle me. I shoved him away and he tumbled down the rest of the steps, crashing into the cops below like a bowling ball hitting pins. I launched down the last of the steps in one move, propelling myself with the help of the right handrail. A couple of the cops, caught in the collision Kelvin had caused, swung their hands out at my feet as I landed on the concrete. I bolted as fast as I could over and away from them.

They scrambled to their feet, weapons raised, but I'd already made it into the dark.

I ran through the carpark, ducking and swerving around parked cars, leaping over speed bumps.

'Stop, police!' came a voice over a loudspeaker.

I made a quick left and dropped to the ground, taking cover behind a parked van. Cautiously, I peered around the back bumper bar and then snapped back immediately. Only a few metres away, Kelvin was striding along in the shadows, checking around every car, but what had made me jump was the gun in his hand! Didn't the other cops realise he was a fake?

Not far behind him, the real police were closing in. They'd fanned out, covering wide ground. Their torches zigzagged over the bitumen, searching for a sign of me.

Frantic, I scrambled sideways like a crab, scuttling from car to car, crouched down, keeping ahead of Kelvin, and keeping ahead of the police. I was tracing the high fence surrounding the hospital grounds, searching desperately for an opening so I could get out, but finally the inevitable happened. I reached the end of the line of cars . . . There was a tree, and then there was nothing but the exposed bitumen of the emptied lot. I'd run out of cover.

The barking of police sniffer dogs approached.

I'm doomed!

I had nowhere to hide! Keeping low, I stumbled across the uneven ground, then took cover behind the lone tree. A few metres away, the fence separated me from the road into the hospital. It was too high to scale. I peered around the tree and saw Kelvin checking under the last of the cars.

Not far behind him were two German shepherds pulling ferociously on chains, held back only by the strength of the two cops behind them.

I turned to Kelvin again. He stood up, looked around, then stared my way.

The headlights and the red tail-lights of the traffic were only a matter of metres away, but the problem was that they were on the other side of this never-ending fence.

The back of the building wasn't far away, but I'd need to break cover to try and make it over there.

I had to escape. I had to find Gabbi. The only hope she had of staying alive depended on my escape. I had no choice but to run for my life and hope no-one would shoot me in the back.

1:10 am

'There he is!'

The dogs barked wildly and the police shouted as I ran, chest thumping, praying I'd get out of there alive!

The sound of a thousand sirens began blaring, and the screeching of a fast-approaching vehicle forced me to throw a split-second look behind me.

An ambulance had screamed into view, speeding up the carpark from behind me. The driver was crazy, almost taking out half of my pursuers as it sped towards Casualty at the back of the building—the spot I was headed.

The manic ambo caused enough of a disturbance to get me safely around the brick corner of the building, but as I continued running, it skidded around the corner, past me, and spun out, stopping in front of me.

I was caught like a deer in headlights.

The driver jumped out and ran to the back of the vehicle, flinging open the doors.

I had no time to waste on figuring out what to do. I'd have to run past him and hope my pursuers would lose me, for a few seconds at least, behind the ambulance's bulk.

As I ran past its wide-open double doors, a strong hand lunged out and grabbed me, and before I knew what was happening, I was slammed against the ambulance. Winded, I gasped for breath.

'Quick, Cal!' The paramedic who'd grabbed me spoke in a low, urgent voice. 'Get onto the stretcher! Let's get you out of here!'

'*What?* Who are you?' I gasped.

'Do you want to get out of here or not? Just do what I say!'

The stranger let go of me and pulled a stretcher out of the back of the ambulance, and lifted up the white sheet that was spread across it.

I hesitated. Was this another plot? I had Kelvin, the cops, two German shepherds, and hospital security chasing me, and now a stranger was offering me eleventh hour help. Before I could make a decision, the stranger grabbed me, threw me onto the narrow bed, and covered me with the sheet. I struggled, but he pushed me down again.

The shouting and barking of my hunters was almost upon us.

'I'm Nelson Sharkey. I'm here to get you out of this place! Shut up and be still if you want to stay alive!'

'Release the dogs!' shouted a voice.

The stretcher started moving and I was shoved into the back of the ambulance. The doors slammed shut.

Within seconds the ambulance, with me inside it, rocketed away.

The yells and cries of those searching for me faded. The thumping of my heart eased. I grasped the edge of the stretcher with both hands as we hurtled away, siren blaring.

I couldn't believe what had just happened! I lay under the sheet, weak with relief.

I'd been saved! By the ex-detective who'd offered me help ages ago on my blog! I'd pretty much ignored him, unable to trust anyone, and then just when everything seemed hopeless, Nelson Sharkey had come through for me!

1:26 am

Nelson Sharkey's voice called out from the front of the ambulance.

'You OK back there?'

'Think so,' I said, finally pulling the sheet off me, and sitting up.

'Where to?'

I could only think of one place—somewhere I hoped I'd be safe, somewhere the police wouldn't think of looking.

I directed him to a spot about fifteen minutes away from where we were.

Eventually the ambulance came to a stop and I crouched beside the stretcher, waiting for the back doors to open. I pulled at the pale-green top I was wearing and fanned myself. I was drenched in sweat.

As Sharkey opened the back doors, I got my first proper look at him. He was a broad-shouldered guy, maybe in his fifties, with short black hair and watchful eyes. There was a half-smile on his face as he said, 'OK, we're here. It looks safe to get out.'

I jumped out and looked around. The street was deserted, aside from a couple of cats hissing at each other from opposite sides of the road.

'Mr Sharkey,' I said, offering him my hand, the dirty nylon cuff still dangling from my wrist, 'that was an awesome escape. I didn't think I was going to make it. You couldn't have had better timing.'

'Like I said when I tried to contact you on your blog, I've always believed in your innocence. Still do. A good detective has a sixth sense about that sort of thing.'

Sharkey stopped talking for a second and pushed the doors closed again, slapping his hands together afterwards. 'I can't hang around now—I need to get this vehicle out of sight.'

'I have to find my sister. Will you help me? I have no idea who has her, and I don't know how long . . . how long she'll last out there.'

Sharkey nodded in understanding. 'It's a shocking situation you're in. And everyone believes you had something to do with it.'

'Help me find her.'

'I'm on to it already,' he said. 'That's why I'm here. To help.' He pulled out a card and pressed it in my hand. 'Call me and we'll meet somewhere safe to talk. *Sooner* rather than later.'

I felt some of the heavy pressure on my shoulders easing. 'Thanks, Detective Sharkey.'

'*Ex*-detective. And Nelson or Sharkey will do,' he said before jumping back into the driver's seat. The ambulance that had taken me to freedom sped away, out of sight.

I hurried through the darkness and up the street, stopping only to pull off the nurse's gear and toss it into someone's rubbish bin. When I reached the building, I rushed to the back and silently headed up the fire stairs.

12 Lesley Street

2:22 am

At the top of the fire-escape, I ran across the rooftop, straight to Winter's door.

I tapped on it softly at first. I didn't want to scare her.

I started tapping a bit louder.

A soft light came on, glowing through a front window.

'It's me,' I whispered. 'Winter, it's me, Cal.'

Another light went on inside.

'Cal?' I heard Winter say. 'Is it really you? Or am I dreaming?'

'You're not dreaming. Open up, please.'

Winter unlocked the door and eased it open a fraction. From behind it, she looked up at me with sleepy, hopeful eyes.

'Cal!' she cried, throwing her arms around me, and pulling me inside her flat. 'I can't believe it's really you!' She hugged me tighter than I'd ever been hugged before, burying her face into my shoulder. 'We were so worried about you,' she said, stepping back to look at me, her eyes filled with concern. 'At the cemetery . . . we had no idea where you were or what was happening to you, or whether they'd reach you in time.' She let go of me for a second and locked the front door again. 'We hid in the bushes and watched the Emergency Services digging you out. They dug up three graves before they found you. Three! The ambulance was there waiting. They loaded you into the back of it and took off at full speed with the siren blaring; that's how we knew you were still alive. But then we didn't know where they were taking you.'

Winter was wearing a white, oversized T-shirt and her hair was even wilder than usual. I was so happy to see her, but right now all I could think of was my little sister.

'They've taken Gabbi,' I said.

'I know,' she said, solemnly.

As I looked around her place, I couldn't help thinking that last time I'd been here we'd all been so full of hope, with the Ormond Riddle and the Ormond Jewel on the table, thinking we were on our way to cracking the DMO. Now the atmosphere was very different. Now I had nothing but the clothes on my back. And hospital shoes.

Winter wandered over to the couch, and that's when I saw a big lump on it covered by a blanket.

She shook it.

The big lump rolled over and snorted, opening his eyes.

Boges!

As soon as he saw me he threw the blanket off, and jumped up.

'Dude!' he said, leaning in to give me a big bear hug. 'I thought I was seeing things! You're alive! I have to say, we thought we'd lost you for sure.' He paused. 'I was kicking myself for letting you down back at Rathbone's. We said we had your back, and then . . . we let you slip away. Winter and I have been here racking our brains, trying to work out what to do . . .'

I patted his arm. 'I owe my life to you,' I said. 'To both of you.'

'So you've heard the news?'

I nodded. 'I just hope whoever has her is looking after her properly. I just can't believe they'd take her. She's just a kid. A sick kid. I mean, she needs to be fed intravenously.'

I thought of Gabbi, helpless in the hands of criminals. Tears stung my eyes. I tightened my jaw. 'We have to find out who has her and get her back.'

'How did you get out of police custody?' asked Winter, from behind the door of her open fridge. 'What's that on your wrist?'

Winter pulled out a bottle of orange juice and some leftover pizza, then handed them both to me. In between mouthfuls, I explained how I woke up in a bed in a secure hospital ward, with no idea of how I got out of the coffin. I told them about the detective, Dorian McGrath, questioning me, and Mum and Rafe showing up, hoping I'd fess up and tell them what I'd done with Gabbi.

'Then you wouldn't believe how I got out,' I said.

'Try us,' said Winter, leaning in to cut the remaining cuff from my wrist.

Boges and Winter listened intently as I relayed what had happened.

'So Nelson Sharkey turns out to be a good guy,' said Boges. 'And Kelvin . . . what was he doing there? Do you think Oriana has Gab?'

My friends looked at each other, then back at me.

'I'm still trying to work that out,' I said. 'Rathbone must be working with Oriana, and the whole thing was a set-up. They have everything. The Jewel, the Riddle,' I mumbled, feeling completely deflated. 'And now, maybe, Gabbi.'

'But that doesn't make sense,' said Winter. 'Why would she take your sister if she has everything from you already? Why would she send Kelvin after you?'

'He had a gun,' I said.

'He was trying to kill you?'

I shrugged. 'What other reason could there be?' I said. 'I was supposed to die down there in that coffin. Someone attacked me at the undertakers' and before I knew it, I was buried. They knocked me out with something, and I don't think they were counting on me ever waking up.'

'Incredible,' said Winter. 'Some people are totally evil!'

'So do you think Sligo has her?' I asked Winter. 'You'd know if he was up to something, wouldn't you? Have you heard anything?'

'Cal, believe me, I've been on red alert, trying to listen in on everything that's been occupying him. I haven't heard a thing.'

'So there hasn't been any unusual activity? Nothing out of the ordinary?'

'Nothing, I'm afraid. But I'll report back on anything I hear that could help us. Are you OK, Cal?' she asked. 'You look kind of white.'

'I'm just wrecked,' I said, falling back, deep into the couch. 'And exhausted. I'm sick to my stomach about Gabs. I've lost everything we've worked so hard on, and now Gab . . . I just don't know what to do next.'

'You know, maybe that Ormond Angel *is* looking after you,' Boges said, after a pause. 'You made it out of the coffin alive, and you escaped from the cops again.'

'If he is, he's going to have to try a whole lot harder,' I said. 'And he sure isn't looking after Gabbi, right now, and that's all I care about.'

'So,' said Boges, 'I know everyone thinks you're a dangerous criminal, but surely they need substantial incriminating evidence?'

'They said my DNA was found at the crime scene—where she went missing. Rafe's place.'

Boges nodded, knowingly. 'You broke into Rafe's that time and probably would have touched almost every surface there. There's a legitimate reason for your DNA to be there.'

'Yeah, I tried to tell them that, but it didn't go down very well. And anyway, apparently they can tell the difference between historical DNA and something that's just been laid down—and that's what they reckon they found in Gabbi's room. My fresh DNA.'

Winter and Boges looked at each other again, hopelessly.

'And of course Rathbone and Oriana's messages on my blog have been deleted, so they didn't believe a word I said about the meeting we arranged.'

Boges's eyebrows were almost hitting his hairline. 'I'm the administrator of that blog. Someone's hacked in!'

'Try telling the cops that,' I said. 'They don't believe anything I say. Neither do Mum and Rafe. Rafe was so protective of Mum—he went ballistic at me at the hospital when I mentioned the possibility of my double. He was furious, thinking I was acting crazy, making up more stories, distressing Mum.'

'A twin would have the same DNA!' said Boges. 'What if your twin is involved?'

Your twin. Boges's words sounded so unbelievable to me.

'So you think I *do* have a twin now?' I asked him.

'Anything's possible,' said Boges. 'You have to get to the bottom of that mystery and find out where that guy fits in—if he fits into the story at all. Who knows what he might be capable of doing, and what his motives are.'

The three of us sat wordlessly for a moment, surrounded by the deeper silence of the night.

'My brain needs more sleep,' said Boges, blinking and rubbing his eyes. 'I think I'll go home and sneak into my room. I'll come back soon so we can work out what to do next. And I guess I'll have to resupply you with some necessities, Cal. Take the couch, dude. Get some rest.'

He patted me on the back as he left. 'We'll get her back, dude. We'll get our Gabster back.'

7:01 am

I was having a nightmare where I was in the coffin, struggling in the dark, trying to scream. Out of nowhere the threadbare white toy dog was licking my face, and the scent that I couldn't identify back at Rathbone, Greaves and Diggory suddenly became clear to me. But as soon as I woke up it disappeared again down some deep sinkhole in my mind, like I'd never known it.

I sat up. It was still a little dark outside and cold wind blew in through the open window near the door. I blinked as the light went on.

'Cal! What is it?' Winter sat up in her bed, swamped in her T-shirt. 'You were trying to say something. You must have been having a nightmare.'

I flinched at the memory. 'It's just the recurring nightmare I have,' I said.

Winter pulled a woollen blanket from her bed and wrapped it around her as she took a seat, cross-legged, on the couch beside me.

'It's always the same nightmare. There's a baby crying somewhere in the dark, and there's a worn, old white toy dog . . . Whenever I see it I get this horrible feeling–like I'm lost, and I'm all alone. Like I've been abandoned by someone who I thought cared about me. I wake up feeling like a huge part of me is missing.'

Recognition flickered across Winter's face. She pulled the blanket closer around her shoulders.

'I've never understood it,' I continued, 'and even though I still don't get it, it feels like it should make sense to me. Like there's some huge and obvious clue that I'm overlooking. You know, when I was at the convent, talking to my great-aunt, Millicent, she sang this weird little song about two children, how *one was lost and the other one found*.'

'Why would she sing that particular song?' said Winter. 'Unless . . .'

'Unless,' I finished for her, 'even her confused mind knew something about *twin* babies. Twin babies being separated. Remember how I caught a glimpse of that old newspaper clipping at Great-uncle Bartholomew's place, about twin babies being abducted?'

For a few moments we just sat there, looking into each other's eyes, as if some massive question was on the verge of being answered.

'One was lost,' Winter repeated my words, 'and the other one found.' She started chewing on her bottom lip. 'Cal,' she said, taking one of my hands, and staring at me very seriously, 'I think your double is the lost twin.'

Winter's mobile started ringing from her bedside table. She jumped up and grabbed it, speaking into it only briefly before passing it to me.

'Bodhan for you,' she said.

'Good morning Bodhan,' I said into the phone.

'It's *Boges*, thank you. Anyway, dude, I'll need a little while to get you some decent clothes and a clean mobile, but I just wanted to let you know that I'm onto it. I'll come round as soon as I can. We'll work out a plan to get Gabbi back.'

Winter took the phone off me and walked away as she chatted with my friend. I was surprised at how well they were getting along. 'Sure,' I heard her say before hanging up. 'Great idea. I'll go halves.'

Before I could ask her anything, she spoke again.

'Nightmares are a strange thing, that's for sure. I used to have this one after my parents died,' she said, hopping back down beside me. 'They're sitting on this park bench—we always loved walking to the park together—and watching me playing in a sandpit nearby. Then all of a sudden I can feel myself sinking, like the sandpit's turned into quicksand. I look over at them for help, but their faces have disappeared.'

Winter looked full of sorrow. She retold her dream like it was a memory of something that had really happened to her. I knew what that felt like.

'Their bodies are still sitting there,' she continued, 'exactly as they were before, but their faces are blank. Blank! I start to cry–it's the worst feeling–but I can't tell if they can even see what's happening, or whether they can hear me crying for them. And then just when I'm down to my neck in the sand and think I'm doomed, all these little birds fly towards me from nowhere. Swallows,' she said, her eyes starting to enliven. 'Exactly like the ones I've drawn on my wall over there.'

'Like your tattoo?'

'Yep, just like my tattoo. So they swarm around me in a blackish-grey blur–they almost look like I've drawn them with a pen–then they each grab onto my clothes with their tiny claws, and together they flap their wings and lift me out of the sandpit.'

'Then what happens?'

'Nothing. I'm not sure.'

'Your parents?'

'I don't know. That's pretty much where it always ends.'

I tried to think of something to say about what her dream could mean, but I was drawing a blank. Just like her mum and dad's faces.

'I'm starving,' said Winter. She stood up and wandered over to one of her cupboards. 'Feel free to use the shower while I make us a tasty breakfast. There's a white towel in there that you can use. Pancakes?'

7:45 am

Winter filled a blue and white Chinese bowl with berries, and put a bottle of maple syrup out on the table. Her place smelled so good, I couldn't wait to tuck into the pancakes.

I ruffled up my wet hair with the towel. I should have felt great after having a shower, and knowing something other than grey slop was waiting for me at the table, but my head was all mixed up, trying to work out a plan of attack to track down my sister. The problem was that I didn't know where to begin. Nelson Sharkey, my rescuer and an ex-detective, was the perfect person to have on-side. I needed to call him.

'Oh,' Winter said as she slid a couple of pancakes onto my plate, straight off the hot pan. 'I should give you my notes, so that you at least have something on the DMO to refer to. Now, where did I put them?' Winter wiped her floury hands on a tea towel and searched through some papers on her desk. I spotted her diary there and remembered the line I had read: *How much of myself have I given away, to get the things I want?*

I was ready to give everything if it would bring back Gabbi.

'Here they are,' she said, passing me some folded notes.

I put my fork down and swallowed a huge mouthful.

'The pancakes are awesome. Thanks Winter.'

The Ormond Riddle

Eight are the Leaves on my Ladyes Grace
Fayre sits the Rounde of my Ladyes Face
Thirteen Teares from the Sunnes grate Doore
Make right to treadde in Gules on the Floore
But adde One in for the Queenes fayre Sinne
Then alle shall be tolde and the Yifte unfold

AMOR ET SUEVRE TOSJORS CELER

—middle french

'Thanks for these,' I said to Winter. They weren't the real thing, but they were better than nothing. 'You're not having any pancakes?' I asked, noticing that the pan was sitting in the sink.

'I thought I'd go for something a little healthier. You finished with those?' she asked, pointing to the bowl of berries.

'They're all yours.'

Winter tipped some muesli into the bowl and then added a huge dollop of yoghurt on the top. 'Cal,' she said, 'you can stay here as long as you like. You'll have to disappear when I'm being tutored, but that's about it. Sligo has no idea that we have anything to do with each other, remember. And he almost never comes round here.'

'Almost never' wasn't quite good enough. I'd already 'almost' been sprung by him once before. I knew it wouldn't be safe enough for either of us if I stayed too long, but the thought of being on my own filled me with dread.

'Maybe I will for a couple of days,' I said. 'Right now there are a few places I want to scope out. See if anything points to where Gabbi's being held.'

'Places? Like where?'

'Oriana's, Sligo's—the car yard and his new place.'

'OK, how about you try Oriana's, and I'll stop by the other two?'

'All right, but be careful.'

'Me? You're the one that needs to be careful, Ormond.'

11:12 am

There was a phone call I needed to make before I started walking to Oriana's.

I stopped at a phone box, not far from Winter's, and pulled out Nelson Sharkey's card. I took a deep breath and dialled his number.

He answered almost immediately.

'Sharkey here.'

'Sharkey, it's Cal. I'm more than ready to meet up.'

Fit for Life

12:00 pm

Sharkey was able to see me right away, so I cautiously headed straight over to the meeting place he'd suggested—his gym.

Thoughts of Gabbi had filled my mind on the walk. Who had her? Were they looking after her? What did they want from me in exchange?

'Fit for Life' was painted in faded blue letters on a translucent glass panel in a timber door.

I was hovering outside, unsure whether to just walk on in, or wait for Sharkey, when the door opened and his head popped around it. Beads of sweat dotted his brow.

'Come on in.'

I followed Sharkey into the near-empty gym, past a few resistance machines and an old guy slowly splashing his way along a glassed-in lap pool. In the far right corner, in a small office area, I could see another guy, with a Fit for Life T-shirt on, talking on a phone.

Sharkey stopped at a weight bench and picked up a drink bottle. 'I'm just about finished here,' he said. 'Be done in a minute, then we can talk in the sauna. No-one will hear us there.'

He swung a leg over the bench, laid back and grabbed onto the weight bar.

I climbed onto the rowing machine next to the shelf of weights. I rocked back and forth, starting to work up a sweat.

Sharkey stopped and wiped his glistening face with a towel, then threw it around his neck and gestured to me to follow him.

The door to the sauna was near the lap pool, in the enclosed glass area. We both changed and grabbed fresh towels from a pile near the door to wrap around our waists.

The heat hit me like a wall. The sauna was

empty, but in one corner, coals gleamed under their dusting of ash. Nelson scooped a small bucketful of water out of a deep sink and emptied it on the coals. A white whoosh of steam exploded up into clouds.

'I used to spend hours here in the early days after I got sacked,' he said, flopping down onto one of the wooden benches that ran around the walls.

I sat opposite him. Already the sweat was pouring off me. 'You were sacked?'

He nodded. 'My boss was corrupt. I blew the whistle. Guess what? She got promoted and I got sacked.'

'How could that happen?'

'Very easily. Look at your own situation, Cal. The boss was on the take, accepting bribes from a big criminal gang, and overlooking their crimes. But worse than that, she was tipping them off whenever there was going to be a police raid. I found out and reported it. But then when the hearing was on, these witnesses came forward to say that *I* was the one on the take and that I was the one who had made the warning phone calls. They reckoned it was my voice in the taped conversations. A specialist even testified that he was convinced it was me, when the whole thing must have been a complete fabrication. Or he was being paid for his "opinion". It cost me my job, my reputation, my marriage. My kids won't even talk to me. It was a complete set-up.' He paused, dabbing his face and neck with the corner of his towel.

'I hear you,' I said. 'I had *nothing* to do with Gab's kidnapping. I have no idea how my DNA came to be left at the crime scene. Except that I was in my uncle's house earlier in the year and maybe I left something then. I visited Gabbi when she was in the hospital, and gave her a Celtic ring—maybe that's where my DNA came from. It doesn't matter; everyone's convinced I'm the bad guy. Even my mum and uncle think I'm homicidally insane.'

'That's why I contacted you, Cal. I saw myself in you. I've realised now that it's too late to do anything about my situation, but I figured maybe I could help someone else. Someone like you.'

'You've already helped me once, but I could always do with more,' I said, 'so I'll take it. I have to find my little sister.'

'I'll help in any way I can, Cal. I have many old connections that may be able to supply information, give us some direction. But it may take time and I know that's not what you want to hear. I think your sister's kidnappers will contact you—'

'When? And how?' I cut him short. 'It's not like I can sit at home, waiting by the phone, or waiting for the doorbell to ring—I'm pretty much unreachable.'

'They'll find a way. They always do.'

'And how do you know that's what they'll do anyway?'

'You must have something they want, even if you don't realise what it is yet. I don't believe they'll harm your sister. She's more valuable to them alive.'

'Man, I hope that's true.'

'But first, I need to know what's going on, and the reasons why you're being chased. I understand why the cops are after you, but I've heard on the street that a very big crim is on your tail, too. I have to wonder why that is.'

'Mr Sharkey—Nelson—it's a very long story.'

Sharkey stood up and threw another ladle full of water onto the hot coals. More steam spread into the sticky air. 'Well, Cal, you'd best get started on it then.'

1:15 pm

My story had become such a long saga. Telling the condensed version took me long enough.

I skimmed over most of the details—intentionally omitting Boges and Winter, for starters—and told him how Dad died before he could explain his life-changing discovery to me, that our house was broken into, how I was mistakenly blamed for the attacks on Rafe and Gabbi. And then how everything spiralled out of control, forcing me to dodge at least two big crims and their crews who've been hunting me down like savage, relentless dogs in an effort to solve the Ormond Singularity and take me out of the picture.

'Without my help though,' I explained, 'the things they've stolen from me are almost useless,' I said, hoping I was right. 'You need to know how to interpret them. I'm sure I know more than they do. I've decoded clues in Dad's drawings, found links between the Riddle and the Jewel . . . Maybe I can use that as bargaining power when it comes to getting Gabbi back—I'll offer myself and the information I have as a swap. I'm the person they're really after.'

Sharkey shook his head. 'I'm afraid you're getting ahead of yourself, Cal. We don't even know who has your sister. Yet,' he added. He must have seen the pained look on my face—it wasn't from the intense heat of the sauna. 'They haven't made contact. Yet,' he added again. 'But when they do, how do you know they'll honour their end of the bargain? They could end up with the two of you, instead of just one. You need an exit strategy. Set it up to make it *look* like you're offering yourself in exchange, but know that it will end with both of you free and unharmed.'

I nodded my head, hoping I'd have the chance to use a strategy.

'What's your theory?' asked Sharkey. 'Who do you think is holding your sister?'

'At first I thought Oriana had kidnapped Gabbi, but I'm not so sure now. She was behind that meeting with Rathbone that cost me the Jewel and the Riddle, and almost my life. As far as she knows she has everything from me, so what would she need Gabbi for? There's nothing she needs to trade for. And one of the guys who works for her, Kelvin, came after me at the Armitage District hospital, and by "came after me", I mean he was there to finish off the job. He wasn't there to negotiate a deal with me.'

'So you're thinking Sligo now? It could be someone completely from left field,' suggested Sharkey. 'You need to allow all possibilities.'

I shrugged. I needed somewhere to begin. 'Sligo probably doesn't know that the Jewel and the Riddle are in Oriana's clutches. He probably thinks he can bribe them out of me in exchange for Gab.'

'Vulkan Sligo is one of the most powerful criminals in the city. He's been a thorn in the side of the system for a very long time. Are you sure you know what you're up against?'

'You don't have to tell me. But whether it's Sligo or de la Force, I have to find a way to contact them. I need a contact in the underworld. Someone who knows what's going on, someone to act as a go-between.'

Nelson Sharkey nodded. 'You sure do need to know what you're doing when you're arranging contact with Sligo. You can get yourself tortured and killed by asking questions about someone like him. The underworld is a dangerous place. You need someone who knows how to navigate those waters. How to avoid the sharks and the hidden reefs.'

I knew all about sharks.

'Right,' I said.

'The problem with using a go-between is that because you're dealing with criminals, you're never quite sure whether you can trust them or not.'

'I don't think I have much choice.' The reality of Gabbi's kidnapping was a crushing weight in my mind, never absent.

The ex-detective looked past me as if he was thinking hard, and his shrewd eyes narrowed. 'I guess you don't. This is a nasty situation. Kidnap is a particularly ugly crime. I'll do what I can. You'll need an alias. How about *Mouse*? Mouse, from Armitage. You're sort of small, preyed on by many, and always running about in the dark. Give me your phone number and leave it with me.'

I'm not that small, I thought to myself.

'Mouse will be fine,' I said. 'I don't have a phone right now, but I'll be getting one soon. I'll call you with the details when I can. Thanks,' I said, holding out my hand.

The ex-detective shook it, and smiled, although I wasn't sure if the smile reached his eyes. His weather-beaten face didn't give much away, but I could tell he was intensely committed to my case.

He stood up and stretched. 'OK, let's get out of here before we're cooked.'

2:20 pm

I hurried along the street, still sweaty and hot from the sauna, deep in thought about Gabbi. As I took a hard left-hand turn, I looked up then stopped dead in my tracks.

I'd sprung a guy spray-painting a tag on the run-down wall of a corner shop. He sensed me there, and then tossed the can and vanished around the corner.

NO PSYCHO

It was the 'No Psycho' tagger!

I ran after him, but he disappeared in the maze of alleys.

The paint glistened, still wet. I wanted to know what it meant. It had followed me around the city ever since I first saw it in the storm-water drains.

12 Lesley Street

9:08 pm

I knocked and waited for Winter to open the door of her flat.

It was late. After meeting Sharkey I went by Oriana's place and scoped it out for a while, to suss out whether anything unusual was happening there. I watched the place closely for a couple of hours but it remained empty the whole time.

I knocked again. She had said she was going to be home, but I couldn't see any lights on inside. Maybe she had to duck out for something.

The lock on the door finally twisted, but then it swung open slowly, like it was moving of its own accord.

'Hello?' I asked. 'Winter?'

Cautiously I stepped into the flat.

'Surprise!' Winter and Boges both jumped out from behind the couch!

'Happy belated birthday!' Winter added, revealing an awesome-looking chocolate cake with sixteen candles on top of it.

I grabbed Boges around the shoulders. 'You both nearly gave me a heart attack! Nice hats!' I added, noticing the sparkly party hats they were both wearing. Once I'd caught my breath I realised that the place smelled delicious, and Winter's table was covered in good stuff—lollies, chips, slices and cupcakes!

Boges cleared his throat and in a deep voice started singing 'Happy Birthday'. Winter was quick to join in and add the higher notes.

'Go on, Cal' said Winter. 'Make a wish and blow out the candles!'

I stared into the glow on the cake and smiled. It sure wasn't a *happy* birthday—I was so worried about Gabbi—but having my friends on my side, and a powerful ally like Nelson Sharkey, gave me the boost I needed to know we'd get through it OK.

I blew the candles out and my friends came over and hugged me.

'That's for Gabbi,' said Winter when she saw me looking at a thick, pink candle that was burning on the desk near the photos of her parents. 'That's her candle. I'm going to keep it burning, whenever I'm here, until we bring her home.'

Inside me, the small light of hope in my mind grew, until it shone like sunlight on a murky pond.

'Thanks guys,' I said, and plunged the knife into the cake.

'We're a bit late!' said Winter. 'We planned on doing this after your meeting with Rathbone, but we all know how that didn't quite go to plan. Anyway, you should open your present,' said Winter, pulling out a small box tied with a bow. 'It's from both of us.'

Boges sawed off huge chunks of chocolate cake, while I opened my card and present.

'This is unreal, thanks you guys!' I stared in awe at what I had been given—a new mobile. It was similar to the one I'd just lost, but a newer version.

'I've already set it up for you,' said Boges.

'The number's written on the back of your card. I've done what I can to make sure you can't be tracked on this one, but it's hard to know for sure when technology's always changing. I don't fancy setting another phone up for you again, so do me a favour and try to hold onto this one, will you?'

9:27 pm

'And now for present number two,' announced Boges as we demolished the cake. He lifted a bulging backpack out from behind the couch. 'What do we have here?' he said to himself. He unzipped the bag. 'Ooh, some new clothes!'

Out came a pair of jeans, some T-shirts and hats, and a new hoodie. Boges pulled one thing out after another, flourishing them like a stage magician pulling rabbits out of a hat. He waved them around before tossing them to me.

'Here's your new backpack,' he said, sliding the now-empty bag over to me with a kick of his foot. 'Like I said about the phone, try to hold onto these this time.'

'One final thing,' said Winter, looking at me sheepishly.

'What is it?' I asked. The curious look on Boges's face matched my own. Clearly he had no idea what she was about to reveal either.

She stood up and twisted on the spot, seeming

unsure about whether she wanted to follow through with handing over her gift or not.

'Come on,' said Boges. 'We're late enough with his birthday as it is.'

'OK, but please don't get angry at me,' she begged. 'Promise you won't get angry?'

'Winter, what are you talking about?' I asked.

'Promise?'

'Fine, just out with it already!'

Winter opened a drawer in her kitchen and pulled out a familiar handful of folded papers. She walked over to me slowly, and placed them in my hands, all the time staring into my eyes as if she was afraid of how I was going to react.

Confused, I removed the rubber band around them and unfolded them. A memory stick fell out from in between some of the papers.

'The drawings?' asked Boges, taking the words right out of my mouth. 'The memory stick! And the transparency!'

'And the letters!' said Winter, excitedly, before turning to me very seriously again. 'Remember you said you wouldn't get angry at me.'

'You'd better start talking and explain this, fast,' I told her.

'I can do that,' she agreed, nodding to both of us. 'OK. So on the night that we went with you to Temperance Lane, and we were waiting outside before you went in . . . I was thinking about how dangerous the situation was and how I didn't want you to risk losing everything. I knew you had to take the Jewel and the Riddle, but no-one ever said anything about the drawings or the transparency or the letters that you'd collected and worked on for months.'

Boges started scratching his head and opened his big mouth to interrupt, but Winter quickly shut him up again with one look.

'As I was saying, you needed the Jewel and the Riddle, and that was it. I had an *opportunity* to reach into your bag and remove the other stuff from it, so I did.'

I couldn't believe it—I hadn't lost everything after all!

'Why didn't you just tell me you wanted to do that?' I asked her.

'What, and completely freak you out? I didn't want you to feel like you were in danger! I wasn't even sure if I needed to do what I did, I just did it. In case.'

'And why haven't you told me this already? I've been stressing out thinking I'd lost everything, and all along you've had all this here!'

'Well, I wanted to, but see there was a slight hitch with my plan . . . so I needed to sort that out first. Before I could tell you.'

'Don't stop talking now,' said Boges. He was enthralled!

'The hitch,' she repeated. 'Somewhere in the craziness at the cemetery, I lost them. I thought you were going to *die*, Cal. I wasn't thinking straight.'

'I thought you were dead, too,' added Boges. 'It was one crazy scene. Winter was on her hands and knees trying to find you and dig you out.'

Winter smiled at him, happy to have him defending her.

'When you showed up here I couldn't bring myself to tell you. I'd retraced our steps twice already, trying to track the documents down, without any luck. But then I went back there again this morning . . . and *voila*!'

She sat down, quietly. Her eyes were wide with anticipation. I could see she was nervous and really unsure. 'I'm so sorry, Cal, I was just trying to—'

'Thanks, Winter,' I said, cutting her off with a hug. I held her tight. 'This is the best present,' I whispered in her ear.

'Enough already, guys, you're going to make me cry,' joked Boges.

'I can't believe it,' I said. 'I thought I'd lost everything.' Gabbi's freedom was in reach. 'Now I have bargaining power.'

Boges grinned widely. 'I'm going to concentrate on checking out Oriana de la Force,' he said. 'Follow her. See what I can find out.'

'Her place was empty this afternoon,' I said.

'Winter,' continued Boges. 'I suggest you keep concentrating on Sligo.'

'I'm already onto it,' said Winter. 'But I might sniff out the books—see if there have been any strange arrangements made, like the purchase of any medical equipment.'

'Good idea,' said Boges.

'Why haven't they made contact?' I asked. 'Isn't that what kidnappers do? What's the idea of this waiting game?'

'They probably want you to sweat a while,' said Winter. 'Make you panic a bit, in the hope that you'll give up more than you would normally. Maybe they weren't counting on you being caught by the cops either . . . it depends on who has her.'

'Boges,' I said, suddenly thinking about my online page, 'have you been monitoring my blog?'

'There hasn't been anything on there worth mentioning, but you should check it out.'

I pulled out my new phone and entered my blog address. Winter nibbled on a cupcake while Boges watched over my shoulder.

He was right. There weren't any new private messages, or any clues on my wall, but there were a few messages of support.

Boges stood up and swung his own backpack over his shoulders. 'I have to run, guys,' he announced. 'I'll check in again soon, OK.'

'Want to take some cake or something?' asked Winter.

'Do I look like I need more cake?' he said, patting his belly. 'I'll answer that for you—no.'

'Thanks again,' I shouted as he ran out the door.

14 AUGUST

140 days to go . . .

10:42 am

A whole week had passed since I'd blown out the candles on my belated birthday cake. It had been the fastest week on record. Time was flying through my fingers and we weren't any closer to finding Gabbi.

I was still hiding out in Winter's flat. I had to leave a few times—when she was being tutored—but I felt safe. Boges dropped round whenever he could so we could all talk over any developments. Nelson Sharkey and I had also been in touch, but we were dry on information.

How can a little girl just disappear? Someone must have seen something. I had three people helping me work on it, and so far we'd unearthed nothing. When were the kidnappers going to contact me? I kept thinking of my little sister, wondering if she was still alive.

Something in my heart told me she was.

17 AUGUST

137 days to go . . .

11:32 pm

My mobile started ringing just as I was drifting off to sleep. I almost fell off the couch as I scrambled for it.

'I have a name for you,' said Sharkey. 'But you need to be very wary of her.'

'Her? Who is she? Does she have Gabbi?'

'This is someone who might be able to help you find out who does. Her name is Ma Little. You'll find her in the parlour at Fortescue House—a big old tumbledown mansion she runs as a pub and boarding house. Go there tomorrow, but be very careful. People like Ma, who run messages for both sides, are often in the *pay* of both sides. That way they can sell secrets to the highest bidder. She can put you in touch with a well-known police informant. I can't do it myself. It's important I keep my mug out of the picture.'

18 AUGUST

136 days to go . . .

7:45 am

'Where are you going?' Winter sleepily called out from her bed as I was tying up my shoes.

'Sharkey has a lead for me. He's given me the name of a woman he thinks can help me out. I have to go speak to her now.'

'When will you be back?'

'Don't know. I have my phone with me. Wish me luck.'

'I can do better than that,' said Winter, climbing out of bed and pulling on a pair of jeans. In the blink of an eye, she had a cardigan and sneakers on, and had her hair tied back in a ponytail. 'I can come with you,' she said.

She swung her bag over her shoulder, then grabbed two apples from a bowl near the sink.

'OK. Let's go.'

Fortescue House

9:30 am

We found Fortescue House after a few wrong turns. It was an old building, needing a fresh coat of paint, down near the docks and across the road from something called the Mission to Seafarers.

From the flagpole over the main entrance, a banner flew with a striking image of a lionfish on it. Above the open doorway was a handwritten sign: 'Reception'.

I looked into the dark hallway and saw floorboards, covered in part by worn carpet pieces, empty tables and chairs by a bar, and a rickety staircase leading up to the second floor. At the top of the stairs hung another handwritten sign: 'House Guests Only'. The small reception alcove was just around the corner to our left.

'I'll go inside,' I said to Winter. She nodded to me. 'You stay out here. Wait a minute—'

'What is it?' she asked looking back at me.

'You haven't taken anything out of my backpack, have you?'

Winter rolled her eyes. 'Should I have?' she mocked.

I stepped inside and walked on creaking floorboards to the reception alcove. The smell of stale cigarettes was thick in the air, despite a strong antiseptic cleaner that was being sprayed and wiped on tables by a thin man who turned around as I entered. There was no expression on his face, nor in his cold blue eyes as he stopped what he was doing.

'Can I help you?' he asked. He made it sound like a threat.

'I'm looking for Ma Little. She's expecting me,' I added, although it wasn't strictly accurate. But I wasn't here to be accurate. I was here to be convincing.

'She's expecting *you*?' he asked, like I was some sort of cockroach.

'That's right.'

'Who's there, Ray?' called a man's voice from somewhere deep in the reception area.

'Some kid reckons Ma's expecting him,' said Ray, not taking his cold blue eyes off me. He clutched the cleaning spray trigger like a gun.

'Tell her it's Mouse,' I said. 'From Armitage.'

Ray laughed hard at my name, and accidentally squeezed the cleaner. A fine mist of antiseptic shot out.

From the corner of my eye I saw movement behind the reception area. I blinked in disbelief when the dark shadow I'd imagined was a couple of tall filing cabinets started to move and I realised I was looking at a huge mountain of a woman.

As she approached the grilled area that separated the reception counter from the rest of the entrance, I saw that she was wearing a tent-style dress covered with purple and white flowers on a black background.

'What are you staring at, Mouse?' the huge woman asked in a deep, intimidating voice, which I'd mistaken earlier for a man's. 'Cat got your tongue?'

Ma *Little* was almost two metres tall, and looked almost as wide. Her eyes glittered in a stern face topped with a big, black bob, so thick it could have been a wig.

'Nelson Sharkey suggested we talk,' I said, approaching the grille.

'Old Sharkey and I go back a long way,' said Ma in her gruff voice, giving me a look I couldn't read. Had they been friends? Enemies? 'Let's find somewhere quiet to talk, shall we?' she said.

I walked behind the huge woman as she wobbled into the parlour of Fortescue House, a seedy area past the bar with a few old-fashioned dark leather armchairs gathered around a fake fireplace. Ashtrays sat on stands near the furniture.

Ma Little stopped at a wide lounge chair, turned and practically collapsed into it. Some of the folds around her waist spilled over the arms.

'Nelson said you could help me,' I said, easing myself into a chair nearby. 'I'm trying to get information.'

'What kind of information?' she asked, sounding out of breath.

'A little girl was kidnapped. I need to get a message to her kidnapper.'

A bemused expression creased into her face. 'You're speaking of the Ormond child?'

'That's right.'

'The one with an older brother on the run?'

'So I've heard,' I said, keeping my voice steady.

'Some sort of psycho kid,' she said, peering closely at me. 'Violent, dangerous, unpredictable, *deceitful*.'

'It's his sister I'm interested in. I have to get a message to the people who are holding her.'

'And you think I know who that is?'

'I don't know. I hope so.'

'And who do you think has her?'

'I have my suspicions,' I said. 'I want to put an offer to them.'

'Oh, really? What makes you think *you* can get her back, Mouse?'

'I have some things that they need. Things that will be crucial in achieving their . . . greater goals.'

'Things?'

'Things,' I repeated, unwilling to say too much.

'And you'd like to offer these items in exchange for the little girl? What do you have? A treasure map?' she joked. Her laughter quickly turned into wheezy coughing.

A treasure map . . .

'Something like that,' I said. 'I also have information that will help them understand any items they might have already. Without this information, nothing will make sense.'

'I may have heard a whisper of the girl. But I don't work for nothing.'

I was tempted to pounce and shake the information out of her, but I restrained myself.

'If it's money you're after,' I started to say, with a feeling of despair. 'Then I'm not sure you are the woman to help me.'

'It's not your money I want. If I help you, I'll collect from Sharkey. You tell him that.'

'OK.'

'What are you going to tell him?'

'That you'll collect from him.'

'That Ma Little will collect from Nelson Sharkey,' she repeated.

'I have it,' I said.

'Repeat it after me,' she demanded.

'Ma Little will collect from Nelson Sharkey,' I recited.

'That's good. As for information about the little girl, I hear all kinds of things here in this boarding house. All sorts of people come here. People who are just out of prison. People who are on the run. People who talk too much. They're always talking about what's happening on the street.'

Her eyes narrowed in her pudgy face.

'Like I know there is some kid with a huge price on his head who's giving the cops a very hard time.' She threw back her head and laughed, making me really uncomfortable. 'Don't I just love it when the cops are having a very hard time!' she cried, slapping her knees. 'And you! You must be wetting your pants laughing!'

I wasn't wetting my pants laughing. I didn't feel like joking around—I was worried sick about my sister. I stood there wondering if this woman would ever agree to help me, or whether she just wanted to play with me like a toy.

Her laughter suddenly stopped. Her mouth was a hard, tight line as she spoke. 'You want me to pass on the deal you're offering? The *things*?'

'Yes. Make sure you tell them that without the information I have,' I added, 'they'll *never* get what they want in time. I'm also offering everything I have up here,' I said, tapping my forehead.

'Your head on a plate?' She leaned back in her chair and laughed again, the rough, scratchy sound ending in another wheeze.

Once she'd recovered, she sat staring at me.

Finally she spoke. 'Give us a hand up, will you?'

I got up and grabbed her hands, but I could barely budge her. She started yelling for Ray.

10:02 am

Ray came running, wiping his hands on his jeans. It took all our strength, with Ma Little heaving and grunting and trying to help, to finally pull her out of the deep lounge.

We slowly walked her back to the reception area. She squeezed through the archway near the counter, calling back. 'I'll pass the information on to someone who might be able to help. But don't forget. Tell Nelson Sharkey I'll collect from him.'

Ma Little and Nelson Sharkey seemed to know each other well. I wondered what it was she wanted to collect from him. I didn't think he'd have a great deal of money to hand over. But before I could think any more about it, I heard Ray's voice shouting after me.

'Hey! I know who you are! You're that psycho kid!'

I bolted. I heard him break into a run behind me, and I jumped down the steps leading out of Fortescue House, straight onto the footpath, head down and running as hard as I could. Ma Little might not be after the price on my head, but Ray sure was.

He was running hard behind me. He was fit and lean and probably stronger than me, but I was running for my life, and Gabbi's life too. My feet were pounding down the street. I had to shake him off my trail, but couldn't see any openings, or lanes to turn down. Ray was gaining on me.

From out of nowhere, Winter suddenly materialised in front of me. She ran straight past me, in the opposite direction, and seconds later I heard a big thud, followed by Ray's angry shouting and swearing.

A quick glance behind me showed Winter and Ray scrambling on the floor.

Winter's profuse apologies and Ray's shouting faded into the distance as I escaped.

11:10 am

I made my way back to Winter's flat and was surprised to see that she'd beaten me back there.

'Poor Ray,' she said. 'Every time he tried to get up, I seemed to slip again. I just kept saying "I'm so sorry, I'm such a klutz!"'

'He almost had me. You saved my skin.'

'Told you I'd be useful. So how did it go?'

'Good, I hope.' I told her about the freaky owner of Fortescue House, Ma Little, and our brief conversation. 'I wasn't even sure if she really was a woman. She was so big and had this really deep voice. Anyway, she said she'd pass on my message.'

'I guess we just have to wait,' she said. 'And hope she comes through.'

21 AUGUST

133 days to go . . .

12 Lesley Street

2:11 pm

More days had passed without a word from anyone about Gabbi. Sharkey told me to be patient while waiting to hear from Ma Little. But it was tough. I was constantly fighting off thoughts that my sister had been killed, or had died because she wasn't being cared for properly.

Winter's search for information at Sligo's properties hadn't turned up anything interesting—no unusual purchases, no suspicious activity.

Boges was keeping a watch on Oriana de la Force when he wasn't at school, and I scoped out her place whenever I could, too, but it was quiet there. Nothing out of the ordinary.

I was in the middle of checking my blog when Winter returned. I'd been trying to ignore the constant news headlines with updates on the number of days since Gabbi went missing—I couldn't bear seeing another mention of 'grave fears for her safety'.

This morning Winter had gone to Sligo's car yard again to watch what was going on from afar. She rushed through the doorway in a blur and flung her bag onto her bed, before plonking down cross-legged beside me.

'I thought Zombie had come back from the dead!' she said, wide-eyed. 'I was hiding inside a wrecked car body, monitoring the place, when this guy in a four-wheel drive rolled into the yard. When he climbed out of the car I almost choked! He was the spitting image of Zombrovski!'

'What?' All of these doubles were sending my sanity into a spin.

'Sligo comes out of the building to meet him, and it turns out this guy is Zombie's brother! Zombie Two! And I reckon this guy's even bigger and uglier!'

I swore, dreading what this meant for me.

'Sligo was looking for a replacement,' said Winter, 'and now he's found the ultimate recruit—someone who's swearing vengeance on the psycho kid who killed his brother.'

'I didn't kill Zombie. He killed himself. The bell he'd swung to crush me ended up knocking him out of the tower.'

'Cal, I know.' Winter touched my hand briefly as if to tell me I didn't need to explain myself to her. 'Sometimes karma takes a long time to catch up with you, but I guess for Zombie it happened almost instantly.'

I stared blankly at the floor.

'There's something else, too,' said Winter.

'Oh, no, what is it?'

'You're going to have to move back to the beachside mansion for a while.'

'When? How come?'

'Sligo said something about bringing over a new desk for me. I don't know where it's going to fit . . . but he hasn't given me a time or a date, so I don't think it's safe for you here right now. I've already talked to Boges, so he knows all about it.'

I started grabbing all my things together.

'Don't look so sad,' said Winter, touching my hand again. 'I'll try and get over to see you whenever I can.'

5 Enid Parade, Crystal Beach

5:17 pm

'Dude,' said Boges, 'I checked out the undertakers' place again, and spotted that casket with all the angels and flowers on it, but I couldn't get a look inside it. The salesman was really suspicious and I had to leave.'

'I doubt if the Riddle and the Jewel would still be in there,' I said.

We were sitting at the kitchen bench, back in the Crystal Beach mansion, devouring hot meat pies. Boges had met me outside so he could let me in again and supply me with a new key.

'Look,' he said, showing me his phone. 'A message on your blog from that guy Griff.'

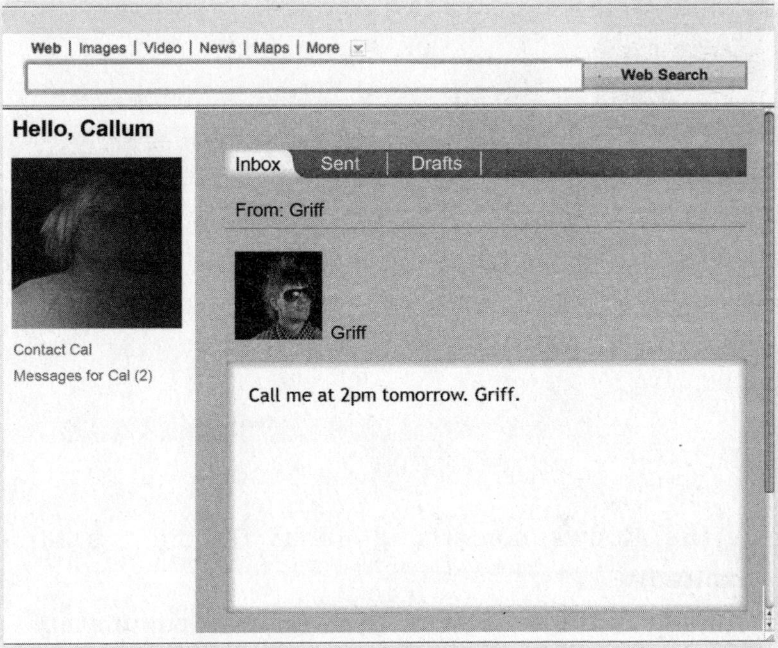

'What the heck's he after?' frowned Boges.

'I don't know, but I can't call him. I don't even have his number any more.'

'I think I might have added it to my phone at some stage,' said Boges. 'Hang on, here's another message from him.'

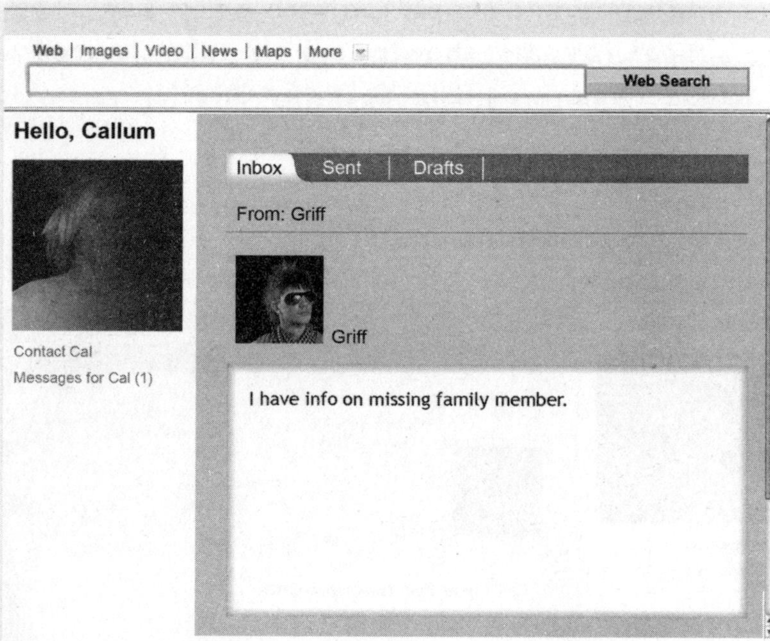

'He knows something about Gabbi!' I said, excitedly.

Boges's face showed that he was completely unconvinced.

'I know I swore I'd never have anything more to do with him, but this changes everything!' My friend was looking at me like I was a fool. 'Dude, I have no leads, whatsoever. Nobody's come through with anything! Why wouldn't I take this chance?'

'Nobody's come through with anything *yet*.'

'I can't waste any more time. Can you please give me his number? I have to find out what he knows. Even if it turns out to be nothing.'

22 AUGUST

132 days to go . . .

Simplicity Guesthouse

4:02 pm

The address Griff had given me over the phone earlier turned out to be an old timber building, which probably once had a view of the sea, but was now surrounded by tall buildings and apartment blocks. I made sure it had a number of exits in case I needed to make a hasty retreat from what I knew deep down was a potentially dangerous meeting.

I found room eleven and knocked on the door, adrenaline rising, ready to sprint if I needed to.

'Come in!' Griff called out. I opened the door quickly and found him lounging on the floor, playing a video game. 'Hang, on, just pausing it,' he said.

He jumped up, a big grin on his face. Above his freckles, his hair was spiked up in a row of peaks, reminding me of a stegosaurus.

'Good to see you! I wasn't sure if you'd really come.'

'I've only come for my sister.'

'You've come to the right man, Cal,' said Griff, checking his row of spikes in the mirror. 'Or should I call you Tom?' he added with a smirk. 'Aunty asked me to find you.'

'Your aunty? I thought she kicked you out.'

'She did. But she realised I'm quite a helpful kind of guy. She's the one who has information for you. *Mouse*.'

'About Gabbi?' I asked, confused. 'How come your aunt knows about that?'

Griff switched off the video game and picked up his wallet and keys. 'My aunty knows everything that goes on in the city. She runs a well-known boarding house.'

'A boarding house? Is your aunty kind of . . . big?' I asked.

'Big? She's huge! Two metres tall!'

I couldn't believe it, his aunt was Ma Little! 'I thought you said she was young?'

'Well, she's younger than my mum, is what I meant. Anyway, she sent me out looking for you to give you the name of a police informant, Dr Leporello. He's agreed to act as the go-between—between you and the people who've kidnapped your sister. Apparently, he will pass messages backwards and forwards.'

'A doctor?' I said. Did that mean someone was looking after Gabbi? 'But why didn't she just pass that information onto Nelson Sharkey?'

'Is that the ex-detective?'

'Sharkey's the one who sent me to Ma Little in the first place.'

'I think she wanted to keep him out of it, until it's time to pay up, of course.' Griff rubbed his fingers together. 'Anyway, let's go. I'll take you to Leporello.'

5:15 pm

I followed Griff along the streets, my new hoodie covering most of my face, hurrying to keep up with him. I couldn't wait to find out whether Gabbi was OK, but I was ready to run at the slightest hint of a double-cross.

'I saw your poster in the cop shop,' said Griff, as we hurried along.

'What were you doing in the cop shop? Caught trying to steal cars again?'

'Just a little misunderstanding that needed clearing up,' he said. 'You realise you're a very valuable commodity—I mean to anyone who might turn you in.'

I stopped in my tracks. 'Are you suggesting you might do that? Because if you are, I'm going to have to take action to protect myself.' I made myself look as threatening as possible. I was a good head taller than Griff now, and much tougher, I knew that.

'Hey! Cool it! Who's talking about turning you in? I'm no rat!'

We resumed our hurried pace, me following him.

'I don't like traitors,' I said. 'And I don't like guys who attack women in carparks, either.'

'Hey, go easy. Don't you remember that I helped you that day? I'm on your side.'

'Really? Still mates with Three-O? Do you know he almost killed me by locking me in a freezer? All for the reward money?'

'I'm nothing like him. Let me prove you wrong. I'm basically a good guy. Anyway, we're here,' said Griff, pointing across the road. 'That's his place over there.'

Dr Leporello operated from a semi-detached cottage that had been made into a small fortress. Steel bars completely enclosed the front verandah—with a steel gate over the front door. A muscly man paced up and down the enclosed area, smoking. As soon as he saw us, he paused, glaring at us menacingly through the bars. He wore a dark-grey charcoal suit, and an open-necked brown shirt, and I couldn't help being reminded of a bad-tempered gorilla in a cage.

'Rack off before I set the dogs on you,' he growled as we approached the steel gate. Some dogs started barking, as if on cue, but I couldn't see where it was coming from.

'We have an appointment to see Dr Leporello,' I called. 'He's expecting me.'

'That's right,' added Griff. 'Ma Little sent us.'

The guy glared at us for a few moments, before disappearing behind the front door. He re-appeared a few moments later and wordlessly beckoned us down a dark hallway.

'Come right down,' another voice called from further down the hall. 'The last door on your right.'

Griff and I hesitantly walked down until we came to the fourth door. It was opened by a stooped man in a black woollen cardigan. He wore very thick glasses, and his long white hair was tied tightly back from his high forehead in a skinny ponytail.

'Dr Leporello?' I asked.

'I am he.'

He ushered us in and we looked around in wonder. The room was very dark apart from isolated pools of light, illuminating botanical specimens under glass. The atmosphere was humid and smelled like wet earth and leaves after rain.

'I was informed you were coming,' said Dr Leporello, waving his hand.

I couldn't help staring at the mushrooms in the glass cases and wondered what on earth he had them here for. He must have seen my puzzled expression. 'I am a leading expert on deadly mushrooms,' he explained. 'Here are three fine specimens.'

On a piece of rotting timber, lit from above, and in a temperature-controlled glass case, three big mushrooms with pale greenish-white caps were growing.

'My favourite,' said Dr Leporello, gently tapping the glass case. '*Amanita phalloides*, the Deathcap Fungus. A very tricky killer. They taste quite nice but after about eight or so hours, you'll get an awful tummy ache. Then you'll feel better and think you've just had food poisoning. Three days later, when you have completely forgotten about your "food poisoning", you drop dead. A marvellous little killer, that one.' He swished his white ponytail around and peered at the mushroom through his thick lenses.

'I've been told you can help me connect with the people who have kidnapped Gabbi Ormond,' I said. I wasn't here to find out about mushrooms. I was hoping this doctor was the kind who could look after Gabbi, but it didn't look like it.

Dr Leporello loomed closer, and as he did, I saw that his skin had the same whitish-green tinge as his three prized mushrooms. Instinctively, I moved back from him.

'My aunt said you'd help my friend Mouse,' Griff patted me on the back, 'get a message to the kidnappers.' Griff's eyes moved to one of the other glass cases, where a huge red mushroom with white spots, like those in fairytales, was growing.

The peculiar man turned to another case, where a tall white mushroom leaned towards the glass wall. 'And this is one of the Death Angels, *Amanita virosa*. Isn't she beautiful,' he sighed.

'I'm afraid we're not here to talk mushrooms.'

'I called my eldest daughter Amanita, and my youngest I called Galerina, after *Galerina autumnalis*, another glorious specimen.' He sighed, completely dismissing what I'd just said. 'You know, I do miss those girls.'

Dr Leporello picked up a piece of paper. 'One must be very careful,' he said, 'when going mushrooming. Every mycophagist needs to know what they're doing.'

'My cough-a-what?' asked Griff.

'Mushroom eater,' he explained, disdainfully.

I was frustrated by this creepy old man with his white hair and his white skin and this collection of killer mushrooms.

'A girl is being held by kidnappers,' I said. 'I was told you would help me. Was I given the correct information, or not?'

Dr Leporello chuckled. My nails dug into my palms as I clenched my fists in anger, but before I could say anything, he started reading from the piece of paper he'd picked up. 'My instructions are these,' he said. 'You are to call this number.'

I snatched it from him and was about to make a call when suddenly the room was plunged into darkness.

'Hey! What's going on?' I yelled. 'Griff, what's going on?'

'I don't know,' he said, his voice just as urgent and panicked.

'Luminous mushrooms,' Dr Leporello's voice came from the corner of the room. My eyes scanned for him. 'Automatic lights. On a timer,' he said. 'Have a look at these.'

On the other side of the room, I could see a greenish glow coming from a cluster of mushrooms. The doctor's face was lit up ghoulishly just centimetres from it.

'Mouse,' called Griff from the doorway. 'We have what we need, let's go.'

I hurried after him.

'What's the rush?' Dr Leporello called after us. 'Where are you going, boys?'

'Getting the hell away from you, fungus face,' muttered Griff, as we hurried out through the front door.

The barking dogs started up again as the muscly guy out front opened the grilled gate to let us through.

'That Leporello guy looks like one of the living dead,' said Griff, as we sprinted across the road. 'Like something from a zombie movie. But at least we have a phone number. You should make that call now. Do you think he made deadly mushrooms on toast for his daughters?'

Before I could answer him, the back doors of a large roadworks van that had been parked on the roadside suddenly flew open and helmeted riot police, complete with shields and batons, spilled out, yelling and charging at me.

I turned, almost skidding over, and raced away.

The street exploded in brilliant lights, throwing my shadow along the footpath ahead of me as I bolted away. Behind me I could hear thudding feet.

'Stop! Police! Stop!'

Head down, I scrambled away, my feet sliding on the footpath in the light drizzle that had just started. I had walked straight into a trap! I didn't know who had betrayed me and I didn't have time to work it out. Griff had disappeared, and that's what I needed to do too.

I pounded back down the road, heading towards the city lights, away from Dr Leporello's street and the riot police.

I could hear them on their radios behind me, giving instructions, shouting orders. I knew that within seconds they could have more police at the other end of the lane—that I was in danger of being hemmed in, with cops behind me and cops ahead.

Shockingly, a loud noise above me filled my ears and the road ahead lit up. Just beyond the approaching intersection hovered a police helicopter, its spotlight shining as brilliant as the sun.

A narrow lane, blocked to traffic with a couple of concrete barriers, offered only a little protection, but I flung myself over.

Crouched behind some garbage bins in the lane, I peered around and watched the road. The sound of the helicopter was deafening. Its light swept over the road that I'd just left, moving over the footpath and parked cars. I didn't know what to do or where to go. Police cars whizzed past, followed by riot cops on foot.

'Search that lane!' someone yelled, so I jumped up, sending rubbish flying, racing away, and praying I wouldn't meet a dead end.

'There he is!'

I finally reached the end of the lane and made a right-hand turn, almost falling as I did. The roar of the chopper came closer and I flattened myself against the walls of terrace houses, hoping to stay out of sight. It seemed as if the helicopter had overshot me, but I couldn't be sure. The ground forces knew my position, so I ran again.

My legs were shaking and I was starting to feel aches and pains all over.

Desperate for somewhere to hide, I realised there was nowhere to go. In this part of town, the terraced houses were built straight onto the footpath—there weren't any yards or gardens or side passages to run down.

I could hear the sirens wailing towards me and the search seemed to be coming closer. The helicopter had turned and was swinging back in my direction!

A truck that had been parked on the street just ahead of me, facing the city, suddenly gunned into life. The passenger door opened, flapping as the vehicle moved along the street.

More riot police?

There was nothing I could do. Nowhere to go.

I was totally trapped.

Then I heard a voice from the truck yelling: 'Get in, dude! Hurry up!'

'Boges?'

'Just get in! Now!' he screamed. A pair of hands stretched out from behind the open door. 'Run!'

I didn't wait a moment longer. I ran for the truck, and in seconds had caught up to it, running alongside the opening where my friend was anxiously prepared to help pull me in.

Riot cops pounded along the footpath in a side lane not far from me now.

'Jump in!' Boges shouted. 'Quick, before anyone sees you!'

With a final burst of energy, I launched myself sideways, getting a foot into the truck and grabbing onto Boges. He wrenched me in with awesome strength and the wildly swinging door slammed shut behind me. This was unbelievable!

'Let's go!' he shouted to the driver. The truck accelerated and sped away from my pursuers. Boges shuffled along the seat to make room for me. I twisted around to see what was happening behind us, and saw a group of riot cops appear from an adjoining lane. They all stopped in the intersection, looking up and down the street, not knowing where I'd gone.

I had been saved in the nick of time by my best buddy.

'Boges,' I gasped, panting for breath. 'You are the best!'

'I know,' chuckled my modest friend. 'But we're not out of trouble just yet!'

I leaned forward and looked across at the determined dark-haired driver hunched over the wheel.

'Sharkey!'

'I had word you were meeting Leporello,' he explained, 'and I just came along to make sure everything went smoothly.'

'Good move!' I said. 'So I guess you've met my friend Boges,' I said, wondering when they'd been in contact.

Sharkey madly wrenched the steering wheel, turning a corner, sending us reeling in the cabin. I reached for my seatbelt.

'Where should I take you two?' he said, veering again to the left, this time to avoid a couple of squad cars screeching up the lane. They took no notice of the truck or its occupants—they were looking for a fugitive on foot!

'Can you take us to the southern end of the city near Central Station?' I asked. Only a few streets away from that spot were the disused railway yards and the big culvert where I had once taken refuge.

'Sure thing. So did you get anything from Dr Leporello?'

'A number I'm supposed to call.'

Sharkey nodded.

'Should he call it?' asked Boges.

'Someone's alerted the police to your position, but I feel confident the number you've been given will be legit. Ma Little's not known for playing games, at least not ones that involve riot police and helicopters. I suggest you keep out of sight for a couple of hours, and in that time call the number. Let me know how you go, and then we should get together and come up with a plan of attack.'

I looked at Boges to see if he wanted to join us.

'Perfect,' he said.

6:53 pm

Sharkey pulled over where I indicated, and both Boges and I scrambled down from the truck.

'Thanks,' I said again. 'I thought I was done for back there. Let's hope you don't have to do this for me a third time.'

7:30 pm

We flashed the light from our mobile phones ahead of us, carefully walking into the darkness of the drainage system, down a steep slope.

'Boges to the rescue,' I commented to my faithful friend.

I could see his grin through the shadows.

'I wasn't happy about you going anywhere with

Griff Kirby,' he explained, 'so I followed you. I let you out of my sight once at your meeting with Rathbone, and look what happened there. I didn't want to let that happen again. When I was hiding outside that Dr Leporello's place I started noticing a few things that troubled me. Like a squad car slowly cruising up and down the street. Like three cops having a deep and meaningful and looking around, as if they were planning something. Another thing I noticed was a guy, like me, hiding and scoping the place out. He matched your description of Sharkey, so I approached him. We teamed up and the rest is history.'

The slope we were walking on levelled out. It was a cold, humid place, with condensation on the walls and the smell of rubbish and rotten leaves.

'I ran in here once some time back,' I said to Boges, 'when I needed a place to hide. I stopped at this spot here.' I swung my light around the tunnel. Above us on the roof was the 'No Psycho' tag. 'There's a small landing space up there,' I said, shining my light towards it. 'I used it as my bedroom last time I stayed here.'

'Nice,' he said sarcastically, before squealing and skipping away from a rat that suddenly ran past our feet.

I looked at my mobile and checked for a signal. I had some reception, so I pulled out the piece of paper Leporello had given me, and dialled the number written on it.

It went straight through to an automated voicemail. I hesitated for a moment, after a digitised voice prompted me to leave a message after the tone.

'This is Callum Ormond,' I finally said. 'I have a number of items in my possession that you will find are essential to you. The information I carry is priceless, and not only that—alone I am worth one hundred thousand dollars. I'm offering myself to you and all the information I have in exchange for the safe return of my sister, Gabbi Ormond. Call me to arrange a meeting.' I left my number and hung up.

Boges was looking at me nervously. 'Big move, dude,' he said, 'offering yourself like that.'

'Nothing matters if something happens to Gabbi. Dad wouldn't have wanted that, and neither do I. I'd take prison any day so my sister can be free. Although I'm hoping to come up with a plan that means we'll both walk free. Anyway, the ball is in their court now.'

I squatted and pulled my backpack off me. I felt totally wrecked.

Boges slid down the wall to sit beside me. 'Cheer up, dude. You need a good night's sleep and so do I.'

The wall and ground we were sitting on started vibrating and thundering noise reverberated throughout the tunnels. I jumped up, alarmed, thinking for a second about floodwaters.

'What the heck is that?' asked Boges, flashing his light around. Almost as quickly as it started, the sound faded.

'It's just the trains,' I said. For a moment I thought of Repro.

'We should get going,' said Boges.

9:43 pm

Boges and I went our separate ways into the night. I was walking along, thinking I'd call Winter and see if she was at home, when I saw someone on the other side of the road at a wall with a spray can. It was the guy I'd sprung the other day!

Roughly my size, his hair was long and light blond like mine used to be, sticking out from underneath the hoodie he was wearing over dark denim jeans and black sneakers. He was tagging the building with a bright yellow 'No Psycho'.

He turned around completely to check that no-one had spotted him, and that's when I saw who it actually was.

I was frozen in shock, and he froze in shock himself!

It was *him*!

My double!

'Hey! You! I want to talk to you!' I yelled out, starting to run towards him. This time, I was going to catch him. This time, I was determined to corner him and find out who he was, why he looked exactly like me and where he fitted into my story.

He took off, chucking the spray can away as he ran. We were almost evenly matched, but he did have quite a few metres' head start and that gave him an advantage.

I kept after him, taking the same tight corners, skidding around, my footsteps thudding along, echoing his. On and on we ran, with him occasionally looking back to see where I was. And I was right on him.

He took evasive action, running up a fence and jumping over it. I copied and did exactly the same, landing heavily on the other side, straightening and running hard again after his vanishing figure.

Soon we were crossing a wide football oval. He jumped a low fence on the other side of the oval and kept running, past rows of houses and apartment buildings. I could see he was tiring. So was I, but I'd had more training in the last six months, and had been well fed and looked after at Winter's.

I chased him around a corner and pounded along to keep up with him. I didn't want him disappearing into one of the houses or buildings before I made the next corner. He almost did, but not quite. I caught a glimpse of his figure running into a tall apartment block and within moments, I was at the heavy glass security door, grabbing it just in time to stop it from locking behind him.

I hid behind a pot plant and watched where he went. He stopped halfway up the stairs—about the third level—and looked down for me. I was hidden from view. He smiled, panting. He thought he'd lost me.

Slowly I crept up the stairs after him, keeping close to the wall. I could hear him fumbling with keys.

I raced up the stairs, pushing myself to take two steps at a time. I flew up the last few and into the corridor. A couple of doors down, my double spun around, his panic-stricken face staring hard at me. He shoved the door open and raced into the apartment, but before he could turn and slam the door behind him, I was already there. I'd thrown my foot in and it copped the brunt of the force.

He vanished inside the apartment. I ran in after him, pausing to work out which room he might have gone into.

I heard the sound of a window opening and ran into the furthest room just in time to see my target leaping out of it. He ran along the flat roof of the adjacent building, and I climbed out of the window, dropping the metre or so onto next-door's roof. I got to my feet and took off towards the door to the staircase. He disappeared into it before I could reach him. I raced over to it, but he'd locked it behind him.

I rattled the door and swore.

I'd lost him.

10:14 pm

I went back to his place to take a look around.

I flicked on the lights and saw that I was in his bedroom. There was a shelf filled with books and trophies and school photos. A pile of clothes lay on the floor, the bed was messy and half-made, and a dirty sock hung over a small flat-screen TV. The room reminded me of my own back home in Richmond.

I picked up a school textbook on his desk. 'Ryan Spencer,' I read, scrawled inside.

He was in the same year as me at school—in the school I'd seen him leaving one time before. I looked at his photos in disbelief. It could have been me, instead of him, posing in the pictures. There was a photo of him with a soccer team, one of him in a wetsuit holding a surfboard . . . and there was one of him hugging an older woman who I guessed was his mum. Even more bizarre, was a small photo of him as a two-or three-year-old. He even looked the same as me then.

I heard a sound outside in the corridor and came to my senses. What was I doing standing here? Any moment Ryan's mum or dad could show up, and I'd be arrested.

As I was turning to leave the room, I saw something on a shelf that sent a shockwave of fear running through my body, transfixing me to the floor.

It couldn't be!

But it was!

Another sound came from outside. I tore myself away from the object I'd been staring at, grabbed one of the photos of Ryan from his desk and ran out of the bedroom. I took off through the front door, into the hall, down the stairs and out of the building, without even checking if the coast was clear.

10:25 pm

I couldn't concentrate. I almost ran under a car, failing to see it until it was almost on top of me. With a screech of brakes, it stopped just in time.

I couldn't believe what I'd just seen in that bedroom.

A call on my mobile interrupted me and my confusion.

'Yep?' I asked, not slowing down.

'We received your message,' said the distorted voice. The kidnappers! I flung myself behind a wall and stopped for a second. 'We accept the deal you offer. Wait for further instructions concerning the time, date and place of the exchange. We will contact you again shortly.'

'Wait!' I shouted, wanting them to assure me Gab was OK. But the line was already dead.

I was shaking all over. The kidnappers had contacted me! They'd accepted my offer!

Immediately, I phoned Boges, but he didn't answer.

boges! kidnappers made contact. call me.

Next I called Winter, just to check it was OK for me to come up. I wouldn't tell her anything yet.

I didn't stop running until I reached her door. She opened it like she was just standing there waiting for me.

'What is it?' she asked, her face pale and concerned. 'Are you OK? Has something happened to Gabbi?'

'They've made contact! They're going to call

me again soon with details for our exchange!'

Winter's hands flew to her mouth. 'You must stay here,' she said, grabbing my arms and pulling me inside. 'I want you here when they call. And you'd better call Boges. He should be here too.'

'I sent him a message already,' I said as I followed her inside. 'But I have no idea when they're going to call again. Do you think Gab's OK? I didn't get a chance to ask them anything.'

'I don't think you should consider the possibility of anything else, Cal.' Winter stopped and put her hand on my brow. 'Are you feeling OK? You look really pale. Paler than I've ever seen you before.'

'Well, there's another thing,' I began, my pulse beginning to slow down. 'Something really freaky has happened . . . and it's nothing to do with the kidnappers.' I shook my head in disbelief.

'Cal, tell me,' Winter gently pleaded, taking my hands again and sitting me down on the couch. She grabbed a bottle of water and handed it to me.

'What I am about to say is going to sound crazy,' I warned, 'and I can hardly believe it myself.'

'You can tell me,' she urged.

'I've seen something from my nightmare.'

'What do you mean "something from your nightmare"?'

I stuttered, not knowing how to begin.

'Take your time.'

'Winter,' I said with a shudder. 'I saw that guy again. My double.'

'But you've seen him before, a few times, right?'

'That's not what has me spooked. My double was spray-painting this "No Psycho" tag that's all over the city, and I followed him, chased after him . . . all the way to an apartment building. He thought he'd lost me, but he hadn't. I got into his house, but he took off through the window. His name is Ryan Spencer.'

I pulled out the photo of him I'd taken from his room, and handed it to her.

'Whoa,' she said, looking at Ryan's picture—it was of him in a red canoe, holding up a big barramundi. 'That's an incredible likeness. And it's so good that you found out who he is at last.'

Winter was impressed, but I knew she was still confused about why I was so shaken up.

I took a deep breath before I spoke again.

'And so in the room—his bedroom—I saw something,' I gulped. 'On his shelf was the white toy dog from my nightmare.'

'You saw a toy that looks like the dog in your dream?'

I shook my head. 'No, no, no, not *looks like*. *Is*. It is *the* dog. It's the exact same dog from my nightmare—worn and threadbare. When I think about it now . . . Look, I have goose bumps! How come Ryan Spencer has the dog from my recurring nightmare?'

I shivered as I held out my arm to see all the hair follicles rising.

Winter stared at me. 'There could be a lot of those toys around,' she said. But even she looked unconvinced that it was just a coincidence.

'How can something from a dream creep into the real world?' I asked.

'It's more likely,' Winter began, 'that something from the real world crept into your dream.'

I stopped to think about what she'd just said. 'So are you saying that you really believe he's my twin? That at some point we have both known the same white toy dog?'

She nodded. '*One was found and the other one lost*,' she said, repeating the haunting words from my great-aunt's song. 'Which begs the question . . . which one was found, and which one was lost?'

It felt like the room was whirling around me. I was positive my parents were my own. I was positive I was an Ormond. I looked like my parents.

Ryan Spencer looked like *my* parents, too.

11:32 pm

In an attempt to distract me from thinking about Ryan Spencer, Winter started showing me through some of her DMO notes.

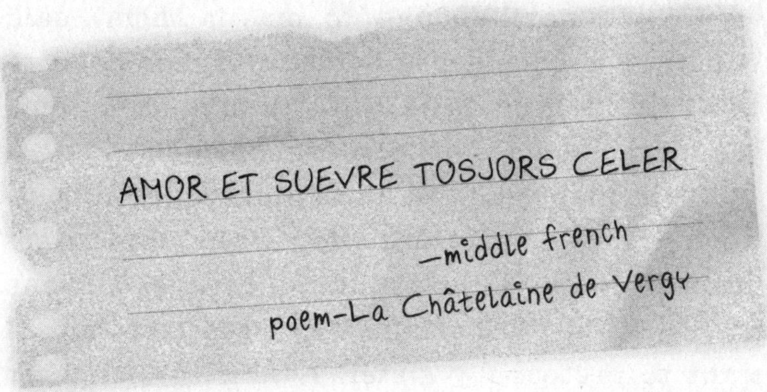

'It comes from a poem called *La Châtelaine de Vergy*. "Châtelaine" is a word meaning "mistress" of a place and "Vergy" is a place in the south of France.'

'First Ireland, now France,' I muttered. 'This is wild.'

'Cal,' said Winter in a gentle voice, 'we're uncovering more information all the time. Once you have Gabbi back—'

'What if I don't?' The thought was too horrible to bear. 'When the kidnappers call me, we're going to have to work out a way to doublecross them. Get Gabbi back safely and also keep me out of their clutches so that we can return to solving the mystery of the Ormond Singularity. And get the Jewel and the Riddle back.'

'We're smart enough to outwit them,' said Winter. She considered something, her head to one side. 'Maybe Griff Kirby would have some good ideas about doublecrossing people.'

I shook my head. 'He's unreliable and untrustworthy. He was probably the rat that almost got me captured after I went to see Leporello. It has to be just us, the people I can trust,' I said. 'I want to protect my sister. I want to bring her home to convince my mum that I'm not a psychopath and I'd never hurt my family.'

27 AUGUST

127 days to go . . .

5 Enid Parade, Crystal Beach

10:10 am

I watched Boges discreetly from behind the heavy curtains. He was walking up the driveway, wheeling a pushbike, and carrying two mop buckets and a helmet in one hand. I let him in when he reached the front entrance, where he dropped the cleaning gear and the bike and came inside.

'Heard anything more?' he asked.

I shook my head.

I had to admit I was losing faith every day. I refused to believe my sister was dead, but it was so hard to get on with life, day after day, not knowing what to do next. Being completely out of control of a situation.

'They'll come through. So when are we going to meet up with Nelson Sharkey?'

'I've spoken to him a couple of times, but I don't think there's any point until I've had word from the kidnappers. Unless, of course, one of us finds something out before then. The plan is to doublecross the double-crossers.'

'Speaking of doubles,' said Boges. 'Any more thoughts on Ryan Spencer? Or the white toy dog? Have you had the nightmare since?'

'It's not a coincidence, Boges,' I said, sensing my friend's cynicism.

'I believe you, I believe you,' he repeated. 'I guess we can investigate that as soon as this trade with the kidnappers takes place. Anyway, I can't stay; I just wanted to bring the bike over to you, help you get around a little bit faster. It was dumped at the tip, but all it needed was a new link in its chain and air in the tyres. Just watch out for Zombie Two if you're planning on swinging by either of Sligo's places.'

1:32 pm

From behind the wreck of a rusty yellow Volkswagen, I watched Vulkan Sligo's car yard. Riding the bike over had been so good. I'd left it in bushland a few metres back.

It was very quiet.

At one point, I thought I saw someone wandering through the piles of car parts. It made me think about Winter again, searching for the wreck of the car that killed her parents.

But I must have been imagining things.

3:13 pm

Oriana de la Force's place had a little more going on today. Sumo was there, taking boxes in and out of the house. I tried to sneak around to the dark blue Mercedes to get a peek inside one, but it was just too risky.

When he had finished at the house and squeezed himself back into the car to drive off, I decided to follow him.

I had to keep up with him, while also staying a good distance away from him. Luckily he stopped at a few consecutive red lights, giving me the chance to keep sight of him.

He first called into a betting shop. Impatiently I waited across the road, by a charity bin, hoping he wouldn't be in there all day.

About an hour or so later he came out, folding a wad of cash into his wallet. He then proceeded down the road, past five or six shops, and entered a big pharmacy on the corner.

I chained my bike to a pole and wandered down after him on foot. Curious, I watched him through the plate glass front window.

He was wandering up and down the aisles, clutching a jar of vitamins. I was about to hurry away, when I saw someone announce something from behind the prescription counter—Sumo responded as though his name had been called.

From a dispensary behind the counter the pharmacist gestured to something in a plastic tray. I edged closer and squinted. I couldn't read what the package said. I needed to get inside.

A buzzer on the door sounded as I walked in. I quickly ducked behind a row of make-up and nail polish, and peered out. I could just make out some of the writing on the side of the box.

Nutrition. Balanced formula. Intravenous.

I'd seen enough. I ran out the door and down the street to my bike. I frantically unbolted the chain, pulled on my helmet, and hopped on, ready to follow Sumo to my sister.

I pulled out my phone.

'Boges!' I shouted. 'It's Oriana! Oriana has Gabbi!'

4:19 pm

An electric charge of excitement went through me. She was alive! There was only one reason Sumo could have been collecting intravenous food. It had to be for Gabbi.

Oriana was one hell of an evil woman, but at least she was making sure that my sister stayed alive.

Sumo walked out of the chemist, package in

tow, and down to the Mercedes. He backed out of his parking spot and drove off.

I pedalled after him like I'd never pedalled before.

The Mercedes was veering towards the freeway out of the city.

A large State Road Authority sign overhead warned, 'No pedestrian or bicycle access'. I ignored it. I didn't know how I could possibly keep up with him, but there was no way I was going to just give up.

I saw the speed limit—110 kilometres per hour—and started pedalling even harder. It seemed like Sumo was going at least ten kilometres over the limit, and in what felt like seconds, I'd lost him. He'd completely disappeared from view.

I let the pedals go and just glided along, sitting back on the bike and running my hands through my hair in frustration.

29 AUGUST

125 days to go . . .

12 Lesley Street

1:15 pm

'Yes, Oriana de la Force is the person responsible for Gabbi's kidnapping,' I repeated to Boges and Winter as we sat around a table at her flat. 'But Gab's not being kept at Oriana's house. Sumo was heading out of the city on the freeway when I lost him, so I'm sure they're hiding her somewhere out of town.'

The three of us were just sitting around, waiting for my phone to ring. It was becoming too familiar a scenario. We were all getting fidgety.

When my mobile finally rang, all of us jumped out of our seats.

'Yes? I'm here,' I said, fumbling with the phone nervously.

'If you want your sister back alive,' said the same distorted, digitised voice from the last call, 'listen carefully to what I'm about to say.'

'I'm listening,' I said, frozen to attention.

'First of all, tell no-one about this. If you do, we'll find out, and you do not want that to happen.'

I looked at my two friends. They already knew what was happening. I hoped the kidnapper was referring more to the authorities.

'Who are you?' I asked.

The anonymous voice continued as if I hadn't spoken. 'Come alone to the town of Billabong. Wait at the Billabong Café—it keeps late hours. Be there by nine pm, and wait until you receive another phone call with instructions on exactly what to do. You must come alone, and unarmed, and bring with you all of the items and information you claim to possess. Do you understand? You must be prepared to hand over everything, including yourself. Is that clear?'

'I get it. But how do I know that you won't just take me and not return Gabbi?'

The voice didn't seem to hear or care about my question.

'The exchange itself will take place on the roadside. You will only be given further instruction as you require it. You will be told at the café exactly where to go and not a moment before.'

'Hang on,' I said, trying to think fast. 'If you're taking me, you can't just drop Gabbi on the side of the road in the middle of nowhere! My sister's in a coma, for crying out loud! The deal is off unless you allow me to bring someone with me. A girl. Someone to collect Gabbi. Someone who will ensure she's taken home safely.' I lifted my eyes and looked directly at Winter.

She read the question in them. Solemnly she nodded. New courage surged through me. I had brave friends.

There was silence at the other end of the line, but I could tell that my proposition was being discussed. I strained my ears to try to pick up the murmured consultations.

It seemed to take ages.

Finally, the voice came back. 'Very well, you may bring a girl along, but if anything goes wrong, and you bring anybody else . . .'

'I'll bring the girl only,' I said.

'And no police.'

I couldn't help but laugh at this. 'You have to be joking,' I said. 'Deal. The Billabong Café. I'll wait there with the girl. When?'

'Be there at nine pm on the 31st.'

The line went dead.

'Dude, I want to be there, too!'

'I can't risk anyone else being there on the road or near the road when the exchange takes place. And surely they'll be watching the Billabong Café earlier, making sure I'm only joined by one person.'

'Well, we'd better start making a plan,' said Boges. 'The double doublecross.'

'Right,' I said. 'Let's meet up with Nelson Sharkey and do just that.'

Fit For Life

2:45 pm

Nelson gestured to us to join him in the tiny gym office. He was sitting at a computer and wanted to show us something. The four of us crowded around the monitor, staring at a detailed online map.

'It's way out west,' said Nelson, as he zoomed in on the tiny town of Billabong, a place on the banks of the Spindrift River, and on the train line, about ten kilometres from the larger township of Melrose.

'It sure is small,' said Winter, studying the image on the screen. 'It only has one main street.'

'How can we make any plans,' I asked, 'when we don't know where exactly the exchange is going to take place?'

'We don't know where it will happen, but we can familiarise ourselves with the location and the general area,' said Nelson. 'Get as much information as we can beforehand and be as prepared as possible so that when we do know the location, we can move quickly and confidently. Exchanges like this are often made in remote places where there is little or no traffic. Let's take a look at Billabong and its surrounding area. They know you'll be on foot, so it can't take place too far from the café.'

Nelson moved the picture on the screen to take in more of the surroundings of the tiny country town.

'That bridge would be the perfect spot,' he said, pointing to a bridge over the river. 'Bridges have been used before for this sort of deal. A bridge can be managed more easily–it can be secured–traffic can be blocked with phoney detour signs. Not that there'd be a whole lot of traffic through Billabong. Let's consider this as a possible site for the exchange.'

'What's that?' I asked, pointing to what looked like another bridge, a smaller one that crossed the river further downstream.

Nelson focused on the small bridge, zooming in on it. Slowly, he nodded. 'This one is more likely,' he said. 'This is the one I'd pick for an exchange. There'd be very little traffic. Looks like it was the original crossing point, before the bigger one was built closer to the township.'

It turned out Billabong only had two bridges, so we felt confident about the two we'd scoped out, and were pretty sure the smaller one would turn out to be the meeting place.

Finally, Sharkey swung around in his chair. 'OK,' he said, 'we have to be ready for anything. Here's the plan. I'll take the three of you with me as far as Melrose. Cal, from there you and Winter will take the train to Billabong—I will sort you out with a fake ID, although you probably won't need it there. You two get off and wait at the café. They'll be watching to make sure you two come alone. Once they've called, you must alert me immediately. By that time, I will have arrived at the Billabong Motel, with my *freshly shorn* son here,' he said, tugging at Boges's lengthy locks.

'Freshly shorn?' Boges scratched his head fiercely.

Any other time I would have laughed out loud. 'Your turn, Boges,' I said, 'for a makeover.'

'It's possible they know what you look like,' said Sharkey, turning to Boges, whose shocked face had brought a smile to Winter's lips. 'So I think a pair of clippers would do the trick. You won't know yourself, and neither will the enemy.'

'It will suit you,' said Winter. 'I'll do it for you.'

'As soon as Gabbi is clear of the kidnappers,'

Nelson said, 'we'll launch ourselves into the scene in a surprise attack. Boges, you and I will deal with the kidnapper, or kidnappers—if there's more than one. While we're doing that, Cal and Winter, you need to focus on getting Gabbi safely into my car. Then we all take off. The whole thing should happen in a matter of seconds so that they won't know what's hit them. We only get one chance at this. OK?'

'OK,' the three of us agreed in unison.

31 AUGUST

123 days to go . . .

7:50 pm

It had been raining constantly for the last couple of days, but as we sat on the train, after leaving Sharkey and Boges behind in Melrose, the downpour eased. I was already cold, pulling my hoodie closer around me, and the thought of meeting the kidnappers in the rain added an extra layer of gloom to my already lousy mood.

Although we'd made copies of the drawings, and hoped we'd escape without giving anything away, I didn't want anyone else to have the originals. Each line had been drawn by my dad's hand, and I wanted to hold onto that. I also didn't want to give all the clues away. Winter came up with a brilliant idea—to make replicas of the drawings to hand over, but mess with them a little. Last night we sat around while she skilfully re-sketched Dad's pictures, but made tiny, subtle differences that we hoped would completely throw anyone trying to decode them.

On the drawing of the butler with the blackjack, she changed the two cards on his tray to add up to an insignificant number; she removed the ball from under the collared monkey's paw; she changed the 'five' in the oval above the door to a 'six', and then moved the dot in between the two place names on the transparency.

I leafed through them. She'd done such a convincing job—I would have been fooled into thinking they were my dad's work.

I reminded myself that even though we had fakes, if all went to plan, the criminals wouldn't get their hands on them anyway. Nor on me. And Gabbi would be safe again. But there were so many chances for things to go awry. What if Sharkey and Boges didn't turn up in time? What if they weren't strong enough to tackle the kidnappers? I'd warned Sharkey that they could be up against all sorts of weaponry, and silently hoped he was coming prepared with his own. I couldn't live with myself if anything happened to my friends.

Winter had taken the clippers to Boges's fuzzy mane this morning. She trimmed it down to about a centimetre and a half. He looked like he was going to cry as he watched his long tendrils fall to the floor in a circle around him, but he looked awesome. I reminded him of how he'd always complained about his hair, and in the end, he was pretty happy with how he looked too—Winter and I both caught his reflection grinning in the mirror.

Now, in the train, Winter sat opposite me. She appeared calm and collected, staring out the window at the evening light on the gentle curves of the foothills. Behind them, the Spindrift Mountains loomed, lightly dusted with snow at their peaks.

I shivered.

8:23 pm

Winter and I got off the train and walked the short distance to the main street. The rain had eased to a drizzle as we crossed the road to the Billabong Café. A pale yellow neon light spelled out its name. I hoped Boges and Sharkey were already there, somewhere in the shadows.

Apart from the Billabong Café, the motel, and the pub on the opposite corner, nothing else seemed open.

'Are you OK?' Winter asked.

'I'm as OK as I can be,' I said, 'under the circumstances. You?'

'Same,' she said, taking my hand.

'You don't have to do this with me, Winter.'

She just smiled at me and squeezed my hand, as if to say there was no way she was backing out on me.

We'd had a few curious looks from locals back at the station, but probably just because we were unfamiliar faces in their small town. I hoped, anyway.

'Am I imagining it,' Winter whispered, as we walked together, 'or do you also feel that someone is watching us?'

'I don't think you are imagining it,' I muttered as we stepped up onto the footpath. I felt pretty certain we were being watched. Not just by locals.

Billabong Café

8:40 pm

We sat down at a table right at the back of the café—in a long, narrow space with dusty bunches of synthetic flowers on vines hanging from the light fittings. We were the only people there, and the owner looked like he was anxious to pack up for the night. The smell of stale fish and chips hung in the air.

It wasn't until I tried to sit still that I realised I was trembling, but it didn't feel like fear, more like tension and anticipation. Winter ordered a couple of milkshakes for us while I sent a pre-prepared text to Boges from under the table.

📱 waiting in café for further instructions.

📱 i know. standing by.

9:21 pm

I tried to swallow some milkshake but my throat felt constricted, as if something was blocking it. I was trying another mouthful when I jumped at my mobile ringing. I snatched it up.

'Yes?'

'Do you have everything with you?' the distorted voice asked.

'Yes.'

'Proceed to the Spindrift River Bridge

immediately. Keep the station on your right, and follow the main road to the bridge on the other side of town. It shouldn't take you more than half an hour. You are to wait there without crossing it. You will be provided with more information once you are in position. Do you understand?'

'Yes, but I–'

'Do you understand?' the voice demanded.

'I understand.'

I turned to Winter and tried to speak without moving my lips and without showing any expression, in case someone was hidden inside the café, watching my reaction. 'They've chosen the main bridge, after all,' I said. 'I have to let Sharkey and Boges know.'

Winter's eyes looked down, indicating under the table.

I punched in the words, blindly, while my phone sat on my knee. I hoped I'd typed enough of it correctly for them to get the right message.

big bridge.now

Leaving our milkshakes almost untouched, we paid and hurried out into the night. The drizzle had stopped, but the night was cold and a misty vapour hung in the air.

We continued walking past the short row of shops and soon we were past the garage at the other end of town and out on the highway on the other side of the small township.

I looked back. Billabong had settled for the night. Apart from the street lights, very few windows of the houses were lit up.

We'd reached the end of the pedestrian foot-path, and had to follow a vague track through the grass by the side of the road.

'If anything happens tonight—' I began.

'Our plan will work, Cal. It has to.'

'But if anything goes wrong . . . with me,' I said, 'promise me that you and Boges will do everything you can to get Gabbi safely home.'

Winter stopped walking and pulled on my arm to stop me. Her eyes looked suddenly worried and scared. She knew she couldn't guarantee I'd make it out OK, but she was trying really hard not to let it show.

'Gabbi will be in safe hands,' she said. 'You can count on me.'

And I knew I could count on Boges.

We continued walking, our breath making little clouds ahead of us.

The land rose slightly and when we reached the top of the rise, I looked down to see a two-lane bridge at the bottom of the incline.

'There it is. Spindrift River Bridge,' I said. Six lights dotted the length of its arch.

'Listen to that,' said Winter, pointing out the sound of gushing water. 'It's the river, running wild after all the rain. It's caught all the run-off from the mountains.'

We both watched the water thrashing over the rocky Spindrift River, metres beneath the bridge.

In the twenty minutes that it had taken us to walk from the Billabong Café to the bridge, only one car had passed us along the lonely road.

The two lanes of the bridge were empty, and we couldn't see anything in the darkness on the other side either. But somewhere over there, Gabbi and her kidnappers were waiting for me.

I took a deep breath and straightened my shoulders.

'OK,' I said. 'Let's go and get Gabbi.'

'But what about Sharkey and Boges?' Winter asked as we hurried downhill towards the start of the bridge.

'I'm sure they're here somewhere, watching our backs, waiting for the action to start.'

'But where's Sharkey's car?' she said, carefully surveying the landscape around us.

'It's here somewhere. It has to be. I reckon they've parked it on that rise just behind us,' I said. 'We'll have the element of surprise, too,' I reminded her. 'The kidnappers aren't expecting a fight—just a couple of kids doing what they've been told to do. When they attack, you grab Gabbi and take her up there, OK?'

Winter nodded, anxiously. 'So then we all meet up back at the car, speed away leaving the kidnappers stranded—without Gabbi, without the information and without you?'

'You got it,' I said.

'They'll come after us,' she warned.

'They may not. Nelson intends to drive Gabbi to the nearest police station for an escort to the hospital. We'll jump out before that, of course.'

Winter looked really unsure. As unsure as I was feeling inside.

'Can you drive?' I asked her. 'If we take too long to join you back at Sharkey's car, I want you to drive the car, with Gabbi inside, away from here without turning back,' I explained. 'Tell me you will?'

'Cal, I can't leave you guys behind. I won't leave *you* behind.'

'Please, Winter, I'm begging you. All I care about is getting Gabbi back. Whatever happens after that, I can deal with. I'm sure Sharkey will have Boges looked after, so don't worry about them, either. Sharkey, Boges and I will be a tough fighting team,' I said, my pulses quickening in anticipation of the ambush.

'And if they're expecting a demure girl who's come along with you to be a babysitter, then they're in for a big shock!'

'You ready, then?'

'Let's do it.'

We stepped out of the bush and onto the road a little before the bridge began. Through the clearing night sky, a half-moon showed and the rushing sound of the flooded river just ahead of us filled the night. It roared away beneath the bridge, in a fast-moving channel about as wide as the highway. Then the racing water narrowed and curved around a bend to disappear into the gloom of the night.

We waited at our end of the bridge. There were no signs of people, other than us. At this hour, only foxes and night birds were out, and from somewhere on the river flats, I heard the eerie shriek of plovers piercing the night.

Winter stood, brave, on my left. My whole body was sweating. In my mind I was chanting: *I'm coming, Gabs. I'm coming to take you home.* In my hands I clutched the parcel they were expecting. I prayed that Sharkey and Boges were in position, keeping up their end of this plan.

A cold, light breeze rustled the silvered leaves of the gum trees, crowded near the riverbanks. Clouds slowly moved across the half-moon, and our world became even darker. I glanced at the time. It was after ten o'clock—and there wasn't a soul in sight.

10:22 pm

A light drizzle started up. I heard a sound and swung round, but there was nothing there. Spooked, we moved further onto the bridge.

What if the kidnappers had changed their minds, seen something they didn't like and backed off? I felt the beginning of a sob rising up in the back of my throat, and I swallowed it down. I should have convinced Mum back in January to leave the country with me and Gab. None of this would have happened if we'd done that. Gabbi would be safe with Mum and me, in some secure location, not in a coma, being used as a bargaining tool by evil people set on solving the Ormond Singularity first. I should have—

My mobile rang, and I grabbed it from my pocket.

'I'm here,' I said to the kidnappers, 'just as you said I should be—standing at the township end of the bridge. Where are you? Where is Gabbi?'

'You'll see in just a moment. Wait right where you are.'

The line went dead.

The sound of a speeding car tore through the

night air from the other side of the bridge. Headlights appeared, approaching the bridge from the opposite end.

'It's them!' cried Winter, shivering beside me. She tightened her hold on my arm and I tightened my hold on the parcel.

The car paused as it reached the start of the bridge, then began crawling towards us, and the middle of the Spindrift River bridge.

It came to a stop and we squinted in the bright lights shining on us. It wasn't the Mercedes I'd come to know so well. It was a different silhouette altogether.

The headlights suddenly went out.

I was desperate to believe that Sharkey and Boges were just behind us, in similar darkness, waiting for the perfect moment to pounce.

I could hardly hear anything over the rushing water of the river—it seemed to intensify to match my adrenaline. The driver, in shadowy silhouette, opened the car door and stepped onto the bridge.

'Stay here,' I whispered to Winter, putting a restraining hand on her arm. 'I'm going to move in closer.'

'Here I am,' I called out, stepping towards them, and waving the parcel over my head. 'I have everything you want. Let Gabbi go!'

For a long moment, the figure just stood there, unmoving. My eyes vainly tried to make out whether Gabbi was in the car.

Then his voice hissed through the darkness. 'Come closer!'

'Not until I see what you have first,' I said. 'No deal without that. I want to see my sister.'

The man turned back to the car. Was he going to drive away?

'Hey!' I called after him. 'We had a deal! Where's my sister?'

The figure leaned into the rear of the car for a moment but I couldn't make out what he was doing.

What was going on? He stepped away.

The car he'd arrived in suddenly shot backwards. The headlights flashed back on.

There was another guy—a driver!

Now, in the high beam of the headlights, I could see a large bundle lying on the side of the bridge.

The bundle moved.

'It's Gabbi!' Winter cried.

'Gabbi!' I yelled, instinctively running forward. In the blaze of the headlights I could see the top of her pale forehead poking out of the sleeping-bag she was cocooned in, and her golden hair shining. She was just metres from me!

Now was the time for my back-up to appear.

A harsh voice brought me to a sudden halt.

'Stop right there! Leave the information you've bought with you on the ground,' he ordered, moving around to stand visibly in the small pool of light from the bridge. 'And put your hands up in the air.' He was a man I'd never seen before, wearing a padded ski-jacket and a beanie pulled down low to his eyes. His jaw was hard, and his lips formed a thin line above his unshaven chin.

'Did you hear me?' he snarled. 'Put the documents down and put your hands up!'

I did as he said and put the parcel on the ground. I kicked it in his direction, three or four metres away. 'This is what you need,' I said, slowly raising my arms. 'These are all the drawings that my dad did before he died. I also have my notes, some important letters and other crucial pieces of information. It's all there. And here I am,' I said, blinking in the headlights, spreading my hands further to show that I meant to give them no trouble.

He stepped towards the package and bent over to pick it up. 'Is this everything?' he snarled.

'Everything,' I said. 'There's no way I'd risk my sister's life by holding anything back. So now my friend is going to collect Gabbi. OK?'

Winter stepped out of the shadows and stood

beside me. She held her hands up in the air, like me.

The kidnapper nodded and Winter slowly approached Gabbi, lying silent on the road.

'You,' he gestured to me, 'move slowly towards the car. And don't try anything smart.'

Where were Nelson and Boges?

I crept closer, unable to take my eyes off my sister. Winter stooped to pick Gabbi up, while I kept walking towards the kidnappers' car.

The headlights suddenly died again and we were plunged into darkness. Even the low bridge lights went out.

I saw a shadow move in the kidnappers' car.

Where were Nelson and Boges?!

I swung back, intending to warn the others and help Winter carry Gabbi away from here, but the ski-jacket man's vicious voice shouted out, 'Move and I'll shoot!'

Winter gasped. I froze.

'OK! OK!' I cried. 'We're not moving!' I wouldn't dare do anything that would endanger Gabbi's life further.

Nelson and Boges! Hurry up!

Almost the second I thought this, I heard the roar of a fast accelerating car behind me.

Nelson's car screamed onto the bridge, headlights blazing!

The guy in the ski-jacket jumped backwards, shielding his eyes from the high-beam brilliance!

They were here!

'He has a gun!' I shouted as the car screeched and skidded to a halt beside me.

Nelson and Boges exploded out of the car—the engine still revving—and Nelson sprang at the man with the gun, smashing him down onto the roadway, the gun skittering out from his grasp. Boges ran to pick it up.

'Watch the other guy in the car!' I shouted to him. Boges held up the gun and pointed it at the kidnappers' car, moving it shakily, unable to lock onto the target's position. I spun around to Gabbi and Winter.

'Get her in the car!' I hissed as Winter lifted Gabbi from the roadway, struggling with her inert form. Before I had the chance to help her, the second man from the car materialised between us.

He ran towards Boges in a black blur and kicked the gun from my friend's hand, before hurling him heavily to the ground. Next he took a swing at Winter and wrenched Gabbi out of her arms, flinging her tiny, fragile body over his shoulder like it was nothing but a sack of grain. Winter tumbled to the ground.

The driver stood tall and menacing, wearing a black fedora, pulled low, and a black trenchcoat.

I lurched at him, but he held Gabbi high, out of my reach. 'Get back, you crazy little punk!' He spat at me as he retreated, and reached behind his back with his free hand.

'Stay down!' I ordered my friends, thinking this guy was reaching for a gun. Sharkey was still fighting and rolling around with the other gunman in a desperate struggle nearby. All my focus was on Gabbi.

'Let her go, you scumbag!' Winter yelled from behind me.

'You want her? Then get in the car and tell your friends to rack off!'

I leapt towards the car, but as I did the fedora-wearing man sidestepped to the edge of the bridge, still holding my sister aloft. His trenchcoat flapped wildly in an eerie, sudden gust of wind.

'Here, catch!' he screamed.

We all watched in horror as he lifted my sister over the bridge railing and threw her off.

I fell to my knees. Everything around me went hazy and I felt like throwing up. I barely heard the splash as Gabbi crashed into the wild river below.

'Gabbi!' I screamed. 'No!' I scrambled to my feet and raced towards the edge of the bridge, climbing up the railing. I had to save her!

'Cal, no!' I heard Winter cry, desperately.

I stood up and dived head first into the fast-running, freezing water, without a care for the jagged rocks below.

11:02 pm

Under the water I felt like I was in a dreamworld. I couldn't believe this was happening. I fought the surge and kicked my legs, finally emerging and breaking through the surface.

'Gabbi!' I screamed into the darkness as the water thrashed me along. How was I going to find her? The river quickly carried me further and further away from the bridge.

I desperately twisted around, searching for my sister. I hoped the sleeping-bag would have cushioned her fall a little, and that it would help keep her afloat . . . just long enough for me to find her.

I couldn't see anything as the river carried me down, just the chop on the flooded river's surface and the banks looming black on either side.

'Gabbi!' I screamed at the top of my voice, half-choking. 'Gabbi!'

I dived repeatedly, finding calmer water underneath the surface. With every plunge, I reached out into the murky blackness near the bottom of the river, hoping to touch her. I was frantic. In her unconscious state, Gabbi would have no chance—no survival instincts would kick in. Once the sleeping-bag became saturated, it would drag her down to her death.

I groped around in the water, but all my scrabbling fingers could find were stones and mud, decaying timber and leaves.

The cold was getting to me. My ears and head were aching.

I made another panicked dive and collided with a large, submerged log. As I pulled myself away from its clutches, my hands touched fabric! Thick fabric! A sodden sleeping-bag!

I had found her!

I grasped around, pulling at it, looking for her arms so that I could pull her out and take her to the surface with me. I was counting on her still being alive!

But I couldn't find her arms—or her legs. I couldn't find her at all. The sleeping-bag was empty. My sister had been washed away in the torrent!

As I resurfaced, a terrible shriek ripped out of my body. I kicked at the log at my feet, and tore at the empty sleeping-bag, screaming into the night air, howling like a wolf.

Gabbi was gone.

She was gone!

I swam to the edge of the river. It took me five attempts to scramble up the bank.

I had failed in everything. I had lost the Ormond Jewel and the Ormond Riddle.

And now I had lost my little sister's life.

CONSPIRACY 365
12 BOOKS 12 MONTHS
JANUARY
FEBRUARY
MARCH
APRIL
BOOK 1
BOOK 2
BOOK 3
BOOK 4
MAY
JUNE
JULY
AUGUST
BOOK 5
BOOK 6
BOOK 7
BOOK 8
SEPTEMBER
OCTOBER
NOVEMBER
DECEMBER
BOOK 9
BOOK 10
BOOK 11
GOT IT!
GABRIELLE LORD
COLLECT ALL 12 BOOKS